WITHDRAWN
FROM COLLECTION
VPL

NOV. - 5 1993

Lily & Joel

A Novel of Life, Love and AudioTapes

As Told to Arthur Henley

TOP OF THE MOUNTAIN PUBLISHING
Largo, Florida 34643-5117 U.S.A.

All rights reserved. No part of this book may be reproduced, utilized or transmitted in any form or by any means, electronic or mechanical—including photocopying, recording on any information storage and retrieval system—without written permission from the publisher, except for brief quotations or inclusion in a review.

Top Of The Mountain Publishing
11701 South Belcher Road, Suite 123
Largo, Florida 34643-5117 U.S.A.
SAN 287-590X
FAX(24 hour)1(813)536-3681
PHONE 1(813)530-0110

Copyright 1992 by Arthur Henley

Library of Congress Cataloging in Publication Data
   Henley, Arthur.
   Lily & Joel: a novel of life, love, and audiotapes/by Arthur Henley
     p.cm.
   ISBN 1-56087-052-4 (hardback): $21.95 —
   ISBN 1-56087-051-6 (trade pbk.): $9.95
   I.Title. II.Title: Lily & Joel.
   PS3558.E49618L5 1992
   813'.54—dc20   92-4418 CIP

Manufactured in the United States

Dedication

*In grateful remembrance of
Dr. John L. Schimel
for his wit and inspiration.*

"To endure life remains, when all is said, the first duty of all living beings. Illusion can have no value if it makes this more difficult for us."
— Sigmund Freud

To the Reader

You may have read the writings of Lily and Joel Flom in *The New York Times* and elsewhere but, most assuredly, you have never heard their tapes.

It isn't every day one meets a couple as outspoken as these two. When they allowed me to listen to their privately recorded tapes, I found them hilarious — and shockingly true.

Nevertheless, they said they were determined to "let it all hang out because privacy is no longer fashionable," and asked me to help them edit their tapes for publication.

This book is the result, a novel based on the life and love tapes of Lily and Joel Flom. It's about a long hot and sometimes sexy summer in the twenty-fifth year of a marital war — and how a tabloid newspaper, an unusual psychiatrist, and some filthy rich in-laws contributed to it. It's full of love and laughter, and it's very personal.

So, thank you, Lily and Joel, for being so outrageously yourselves.

And thanks, also, to that wonderful gang at *Tomorrow*, especially Max Levin and Harold Drucker the publisher; to Dr. Abel for his jocund insights into the human condition; and to all the family members on whom Joel eavesdropped so shamelessly!

Arthur Henley

I, Lily Flom, reluctantly accuse my beloved husband Joel of harboring passions that have no business in a civilized marriage. It took me twenty-five years to come to this conclusion.

Oh, there were clues dropped here and there, like bird droppings. But you know how it is with bird droppings. You never notice them until they hit you where it counts. Well, soon after Labor Day, on a sweltering hot night, they did just that.

Joel and I were in bed, the same queen-size bed we've shared for twenty-five years. The air-conditioner was going full blast because the THI was 88, a gross temperature humidity index.

Neither heat nor humidity bothers me especially but they do bother Joel. Everything bothers Joel. How much so I was not to discover until after our orgy.

Frankly, I find this so embarrassing to relate that I'm able to do so only after having doubled my usual go-to-sleep dose of *Valium*.

I have always tried to act like a lady and Joel has always treated me like one. Speaking sexually, as people do nowadays, it's been my fashion to intercourse like a lady and he like a gentleman. So we enjoyed what I thought was a beautiful wholesome relationship, like in the storybooks. I was soon to learn that I had been misled. Shockingly misled.

You see, I hadn't counted on Dr. Abel, Joel's dirty-minded analyst. He began to share our bed. Not actually, of course, just in Joel's head. It's what the French call a ménage-à-trois, and yet all three of us are Jewish.

To me this is sacrilegious. Not to Joel. On that eventful night he yanked me into bed with unbecoming zest. I had to remind him he'd forgotten to turn off the light.

"I didn't forget," he said. "I want to leave the light on so I can see what I'm doing."

"After twenty-five years you still don't know what you're doing?"

"I've become more sensual."

"You've become disgusting. Turn off the light and stop acting like a Peeping Tom."

"No!"

"Sssshhhh!"

"What's sssshhhh?"

"You're raising your voice, Joel. We don't need the neighbors to hear."

"Let 'em hear. They'll be so jealous they'll think we're perverts."

"Ah, so now you admit that what we're doing is wrong!"

"Stop talking, Lily, and just react."

"What's going on? I can feel your hands all over me."

"My loving hands."

"Not there, Joel, not there!"

"Yes, here, there and everywhere. All of a sudden you're so self-conscious? You were never self-conscious even before we were married."

"Before we were married, our relationship wasn't sanctified by Jewish law."

"Guilt guilt guilt."

"I'm not going to an analyst. You are."

"It's for you I go. For our marriage, our sex life, our children's sake."

"That's what your Dr. Abel tells you?"

"He doesn't tell me anything."

"So what do you need him for?"

"To help me make my own decisions."

"I've never known you not to make your own decisions."

"Lily, I'm not doing what I'm doing to talk about Dr. Abel."

"Oooh... oooooh... ooooohhhhhhhhh!"

"Ahhhh..."

"Oh my God, I've been raped. I feel like a whore."

"Poor Lily. Here I am all filled up with love and..."

"Wait a minute! What's that noise under the bed, like a ping?"

"Oh, the tape has probably run out."

"What? You're taping us? You have a tape recorder under our bed?"

"It's no big deal. I thought it would be fun listening to the playback."

"The playback?"

"You bet. Think how exciting it'll be to hear ourselves making love."

"I can't believe what I'm hearing."

"Wait'll you hear the tape."

"Was this Dr. Abel's idea? Tell me the truth, Joel!"

"Well, not exactly. He just figured from the things I tell him about us that we say some funny things."

"Funny? He finds our sex life funny?"

"You don't know Dr. Abel, Lily. He has this great ability to see the humor in human relationships."

"Especially ours, you mean."

"Right. That's why he suggested I keep a tape recorder running when we talk."

"We weren't talking, we were fucking."

"Right again. But we were also talking at the same time."

"And you taped our love life for Dr. Abel to hear?"

"Certainly not! I'd be crazy to waste my analytic hour playing tapes for Dr. Abel. I did it for us, so we can listen and re-live these moments."

"You're a degenerate."

"Oh, Lily, you miss the whole point. This is therapy for my mental health."

"I can't believe it. You're using my body to improve your sick mind. When did you start taping us?"

"At the beginning of summer. But it's not just us. I also taped the family, and people at my office."

"You've been bugging everybody? How many tapes do you have?"

"I don't know exactly, but enough to fill a book."

"Book? You intend to expose our private life in a book? No shit? You really mean to do this, Joel?"

"Don't be so crude, Lily. It isn't like you."

"If I'm crude, there's a reason. A book. You really mean to put us in a book, hah?"

"Dr. Abel says that seeing things in print can help us understand each other better. Dr. Abel said..."

"Enough! Don't mention that pervert's name to me again. I'm sorry I had an orgasm."

"Oh, that's priceless, Lily. I wish the tape was still running to capture those words, the tone of your voice, the wonderful way you have of expressing your feelings."

"What do you care about my feelings? All you care about is yourself. And at my expense. But I can't believe you're really serious about revealing our intimate relationship in a book!"

No, I couldn't believe it then, and I can't now. Which brings me back to what I was saying originally about Joel's peculiar passions. He took his tapes, had them transcribed, and added a few comments here and there. Then he convinced me that it should be published as a book because it's very contemporary and the right thing to do.

In the end, I had to agree. After all, anyone who's anybody is making a public confession these days. Why not us? At least what Joel and I have to say makes sense, not headlines. And after twenty-five years of marriage, what's left to be ashamed of?

Besides, Dr. Abel is in the book too, and so are all the crazies at the tabloid where Joel worked, as well as our whole family.

I admit, sometimes I have second thoughts about this project. But it doesn't pay to be disagreeable, especially if you're married to a sick man.

Go on, Joel, play your tapes...

Now that Lily has divulged my secret, I, Joel Flom, want to reassure my darling wife that my recording of our relationship was not done out of maliciousness but out of love. It is an exquisite love, granted to few couples... married or single, living or dead.

Of course, so rich a relationship is not without its psychological pitfalls, as Dr. Abel so aptly points out in this narrative. And since both Lily and I were raised by mothers of the old school who looked upon wives as helpless creatures and husbands as meal tickets, Dr. Abel's influence upon our relationship — as well as Levin's, my boss at the tabloid, *Tomorrow* — cannot be overlooked.

I have taken both influences into account in these tapes. They were made at home, at Dr. Abel's office (with permission), and at the tabloid (without permission, the recorder hidden in a desk drawer). My few bits of commentary are based on careful notes I made and

Lily & Joel

are included to connect one taped episode with another... and to explain what went on in my head.

I dedicate this confessional to all the lunatic lovers who may not realize how much they have in common with Lily and me. This is my story, but actually it has less to do with me than with Lily whom I have loved and hated with equal fervor, as she has me. When she was loving, I was hating, and when she was hating, I was loving. We always agreed, but never in unison. That was the secret of our togetherness.

A paradox.

I have to admit I'm baffled as to how our marriage has survived these twenty-five years. Was it my treatment by Dr. Abel that kept the marriage going, or is it the marriage that kept the treatment going?

Another paradox. This story is full of paradoxes.

I do know that every summer things get worse. When the sun shines fiercely hot and the humidity starts climbing, the soaring THI wreaks havoc on the brain cells. Lily becomes more unpredictable. I become more anxious and my need for treatment rises along with the THI.

Last summer was, in Dickensian terms, "the best of times, the worst of times." It brought forth in passionate abundance both the seeds and the fruit of our exuberant discontent.

On a particular morning early in July, when this tale begins, the THI was peaking at an intolerable high...

approaching 90. Worse still, the air-conditioner had broken down.

To get some relief, I had taken a cooling bath. Upon emerging from the briefly bracing water, I went naked into the living room for some cool corner to dry off in.

Lying lazily on the sofa reading *The New York Times* was Lily, her sun-browned body in stark contrast to my pale skin. She loves the sun, I hate it. Lily turned and gazed upon my nakedness.

"You're ugly," she said.

"I'm hot."

"Put something on, Joel."

"You're only wearing a bra and panties."

"So? I'll get my robe."

"No, no, I like to look at you the way you are."

"You have no shame."

"How beautiful you look. That great brown skin of yours. Every feature. I feel so moved I could rape you."

"See, that's you! That's what you do to something beautiful. You rape it."

"Don't take everything so literally."

"You're a dirty old man, Joel."

"I'm not dirty and I'm not old. I've only just turned fifty."

"You look older."

"If I look older, it's from living with you."

"It's because you smoke and drink and eat candy."

"Goodbye."

"Where are you going? It's your day off."

15

"I'm going to my analyst."

"Today?"

"I need all the treatment I can get to keep myself together. And he's leaving on vacation soon."

"When?"

"At the end of the month. I'd like to get in a few extra sessions if he has the time."

"If you have the money, he'll have the time."

"Don't say that, Lily."

"You're going to report on me!"

"That isn't true."

"I can't wait for him to go on vacation. When is he coming back?"

"Not 'til after Labor Day."

"Good! I'll have you crazy by then."

With my analyst out of the way, she had me at her mercy. And yet every August our vigorous give-and-take was all that kept me going until my treatment could be resumed. What a paradox!

Before I put on my socks, I made notes. Dr. Abel had to know what I was going through.

Dr. Abel's brownstone house in Greenwich Village was like a second home to me. The basement apartment was set up as a waiting room and office; the door connecting the two was soundproofed. Once the door closed behind me, I had him all to myself.

I slumped down into the easy chair and turned on my tape recorder. He nodded approvingly.

"So?"

"I don't know where to begin, doctor. Everything is getting worse."

"You said that last time."

"This time I mean it. Would you please turn up the air-conditioning?"

"It's as high as it will go."

"That's how they make everything these days. Nothing works like it should."

"Why are you so agitated, Mr. Flom?"

"I don't know. Maybe it's the THI. Oomp oomp oomp."

"What's that oomp oomp oomp?"
"Nothing. It's only a grunt."
"Three grunts. A magic number."
"Magic? I should only be so lucky. All my friends think I'm normal so they come to me for advice. But I have to come to you."
"I'm deeply grateful. But remember, you always have Lily to turn to."
"Lily? She contradicts everything I say. She insults me. This morning she told me I'm ugly. She's always telling me I don't make enough money. She keeps pointing an accusing finger at me. 'Another piece of candy is missing!' 'I counted the cigarettes and half the pack is gone!' Things like that."
"You're getting all worked up."
"And with good reason! You know what the trouble is, doctor? She thinks she's a free spirit but she's really very rigid. When it comes to sex, you know what she does? With her lipstick, she makes little red marks on the bed sheet to mark the positions we should take. Cue marks, like we were on the stage!"
"Well, maybe it's the actress in her. She's going to perform."
"That doesn't make sense."
"Few things in life do."
"I tell you, I can't stand it any more!"
"Do you want to leave her?"
"Absolutely!"
"Okay, you've solved your problem."

"How can I leave her? My mother would be heartbroken. My kids would never forgive me... Besides, what if she's right?"

"Ah, so you agree with her criticism of you."

"I don't exactly agree with her when I talk to her but I have to agree with a lot of what she says. After all, I'm not really handsome like Robert Redford, for example. And I'm certainly not a millionaire."

"You feel you've let her down because you aren't Robert Redford or a millionaire."

"Well, I suppose so, from her point of view."

"How about your point of view?"

"I can't stand her demands! I can't help it if I'm not what she'd like me to be. Why doesn't she understand that?"

"Ask her."

"I'll never get a straight answer. That's the trouble with our marriage. We don't communicate."

"You communicate too much."

"Oomp oomp oomp."

"There you go again."

"I have to admit it. Sometimes I hate that woman! Oomp oomp oomp."

"You can't bear to say it so you make those magical grunts to take back what you said."

"Even thinking like that makes me grunt."

"Words, thoughts, deeds, grunts. They're all the same to you. But nothing has really happened. You only told *me* what you thought, not your wife."

"Oh my God, never!"

Dr. Abel laughed, then half-apologized.

"Forgive me, Mr. Flom, but I'm only trying to suggest that you're over-reacting. I want to help you understand that what you see as tragic can really be seen as laughable."

"Why do I see everything as tragic?"

"Because you're suffering from the *Gevolt* syndrome."

"*Gevolt?* What does that mean?"

"It means that everything with you is *Oy Gevolt!* The world is always coming to an end."

"That's ridiculous."

"Now you're making progress."

"But maybe that is the way I really feel. Lots of times, when I open my eyes in the morning, I think to myself, 'All good things must come to an end. I'm awake.'"

"Ah, so even the first thing in the morning it's *Oy Gevolt!*"

"Well, who knows what the day will bring?"

Friday is the most welcome day of the week to anyone who holds a steady job. It means payday and freedom for the next forty-eight hours. But to me it meant none of these things. As a freelance writer living precariously, Friday was just another day in the week, until I joined the staff of the tabloid called *Tomorrow*.

The name was really meaningless since the weekly paper contained only rehashed news features glossied up with big headlines and lots of pictures of celebrities and assorted crazies. It made a mint of money for the publisher, Harold Drucker, an old college chum, who considers it the world's greatest newspaper because, as he has often boasted, "The writing is simple, to the point, and full of cliches that people love because they've heard them before."

He had always wanted me to work for him and I had always graciously declined, not wanting any part of a nine-to-five job. This summer, however, he asked if I would fill in for vacationing staffers — and since times were changing and circulation was dropping, perhaps the sheet could profit from a little more respectability that my own particular writing experience could give it. So my friend, the publisher, offered me a handsome sum and an air-conditioned ambience that would overcome the baleful effects of the THI.

"Take the job," Dr. Abel had advised. "It will keep you cool, keep you solvent, and keep you out of your apartment eight hours a day."

"Lily thinks I'll become tainted."

"The weekly paycheck will soothe her sense of moral outrage. Good luck, and don't forget to bring along your tape recorder."

So I took his advice and took the job, moving from desk to desk to replace a vacationing writer or editor. The chief editor, Max Levin, better known as just plain Levin, is a brilliant newsman of the old school and the acknowledged dean of tabloid journalism. In the massive newsroom, he relishes presiding over a roomful of reporters who respond robot-like to his authority and who share his views on the need for sensational headlines and end-of-the-world type to lure readers.

Knowing that I was a friend of the publisher, he disliked me at once. I got that message on my first day on the job. After planting my tape recorder in a partially opened desk drawer, I merrily pounded out my first story and handed it to him. He threw it in the wastebasket without a word.

"Excuse me," I said, trying to hide my humiliation, "but what's wrong?"

"This isn't the *The New York Times*."

"I know."

"No, you don't."

"With that story, this paper can win a Pulitzer prize."

"A Pulitzer prize doesn't sell five newspapers. Try to remember, Flom, you're a newspaperman now, not a journalist. You're supposed to be writing a story about a cure for arthritis."

"It's not a cure. There is no cure for arthritis. It's about a new drug that isn't even available yet but that medical researchers think may help ease pain."

"Let me teach you something, Flom. When you do a medical story like this, maybe it doesn't mean a cure exactly. But at least it's a breakthrough or a miracle drug, see? Stay away from words like 'may' and 'could.' Use 'can' and 'will.' For impact."

"You mean you want me to lie?"

"There's a fine distinction between lying and playing a little loose with the truth. I don't mind being a little loose with the truth. But outright lies, no. That would affect our credibility. Do you understand?"

"I'm learning."

"Good. Try to remember that our job is to bring our readers hope. Week after week. Hope! This is no doomsday sheet like the *Times*. We can't afford to be dull."

"But don't we have to keep to the facts?"

"Facts are dull. Our job is to embellish the facts."

"I understand, but I want you to know that the only reason I got this story is because the p.r. guy at the medical center is a friend of mine. He was reluctant to deal with a tabloid."

"Never call it a tabloid. Call it a family weekly. And remind them that it's sold in all the supermarkets."

"I don't want my friends to think I'm ashamed of working for a tabloid."

"Why should you be ashamed? Just don't call it one. Then you'll feel as proud as I do."

Before I could answer, one of the reporters called out, "Levin, I got a guy on the phone who says he's blind, has one leg, no fingers and is speaking to me through a tube in his throat. Should I take the story?"

"Sounds like a natural! Make sure you get a picture of the guy. It'll make a great inspirational feature."

I went back to my typewriter and rewrote the piece to Levin's specifications. Every time I pounded a key, I had the eerie feeling that it was somebody else, not me, at the typewriter. And that's how it went for my whole first week at *Tomorrow*.

Like everybody else, I was glad when it was Friday. I could hardly wait to pick up my paycheck and hand it to Lily.

I awoke Saturday morning feeling like I'd been let out of a cage. It was a delicious feeling. The air-conditioner was humming and the opiate receptors in my brain were still effectively keeping the demons at bay.

There in the kitchen by the range stood Lily, looking splendid in the morning light. She seemed so vulnerable that I rushed to her side like a saviour.

"Don't come any closer," she said, "or you'll get some boiling coffee on your body."

"Now you're back to being your old self again. You weren't like this yesterday when I brought home my paycheck."

"That was yesterday. Sit down, Joel, and have breakfast."

I took a sip of coffee.

"Pfeh!"

"What's the matter?"

"There's *Ajax* on the rim of the cup! You didn't rinse it properly."

"Don't be so fussy. Learn to be casual."

"Give me a glass of water quick please!"

"Here."

"That's not a glass. It's a jar."

"If I can't put my hand on a glass, I use something else. I make do."

"One of these mornings, Lily, I'll find you sipping coffee from a pail."

"Here you are, Joel, coffee the way you like it, in your very own mug untouched by any lips except your own."

"Thank you. Now let's discuss the weekend. What are we going to do?"

"We aren't going to do anything. I invited your mother over."

"That was very thoughtful."

"I didn't think she'd come. That's why I asked her."

"You know she doesn't have any place else to go since my father died. When is she coming?"

"When we pick her up. She said she'll be ready at two o'clock but I know she won't."

"Maybe she will."

"She's always late. I went to pick her up last week to go shopping at one, and at two she was still dressing."

"Why don't you tell her you'll be there a half-hour earlier? So if we want her to be ready today at two, tell her we'll be there at one-thirty and she'll be ready by two."

"No, she won't. When we get there, that's when she'll start dressing."

I didn't feel like arguing. I finished breakfast, got dressed, and put a fresh cassette into my tape recorder. A few minutes before two o'clock, we drove over to pick up my mother who lived just a few miles away. I went up to her apartment, leaving Lily downstairs in the car.

While waiting for my mother to finish dressing, I tried to make conversation. Picking up one of her favorite antiques, I said, "This is a beautiful old cigarette box."

"I know. It's over a hundred years old. That's real jade and solid brass, with all hand engraving. There used to be a hinge on it."

"I remember. I used to play with it when I was a kid."

"Yes. That's when it happened."

We finally came downstairs and got into the car. Lily moved to the backseat so my mother could sit up front. I started the motor and we were off.

Suddenly my mother exclaimed, "Look, there's a truck marked 'Explosives'!"

"It's nothing to worry about. Don't be nervous."

"Who's nervous? I just happened to see the sign on the truck."

"It's parked all the way across the street. It's nothing to worry about."

"You know, Joel, you're very peculiar. You make so much of everything."

Lily & Joel

I was lucky to find a parking spot just outside our apartment house. I raced around to the other side of the car to make sure my mother didn't trip getting out. I couldn't wait to get her into our apartment safe and sound.

Besides, the heat and humidity were unbearable and I feared having an anxiety attack. Things got worse when we came inside and Lily said to my mother, "I see you're wearing your new shoes. How do they feel?"

"Very good. Very comfortable. But I think they're too big."

"I thought they felt comfortable."

"They do."

"Then they can't be too big."

"Well, they have to be big to be comfortable."

Lily could never let well enough alone! As usual, I was caught between two mighty opposing forces — my wife and my mother. And how could I go against my mother!

It got even worse when we sat down to dinner. Lily had made cauliflower and was spooning it liberally on my mother's plate.

"Don't give her so much cauliflower," I said in a hoarse whisper. "You know it's hard to chew and she has trouble swallowing."

"All right, I'll take it off her plate."

"No, no, not all of it. Just pick out the hard parts."

I died. It's a terrible thing to know that your mother has an eating problem because of a little throat and a hiatal hernia, while your wife scoffs at such biological shortcomings as absurd.

Keeping a close eye on my mother to see that she swallowed properly was making me a nervous wreck. And I had to turn down the air-conditioner because she was so sensitive to cold air.

While I kept a watchful eye on my mother, Lily kept a watchful eye on me. She took me aside when my mother went to the bathroom and said, "Go break some dishes, Joel. It will make you feel better."

"Don't be ridiculous."

"It's good therapy. And it's cheaper than going to a shrink."

"You compare breaking dishes with psychoanalysis?"

"Why not? You get relief."

"The purpose of analysis is to give insight, real relief. Dr. Abel helps me see through my neurosis by showing me how ludicrous it is. From that comes insight."

"If you live long enough. As far as I'm concerned, your Dr. Abel hasn't done very well by you, and you can tell him I said so."

Oh, would I! Lily could count on that.

When someone tells me to do something, I do it. No questions asked. When I was a little boy playing stickball after school and my mother yelled to me from the porch, "Joel, go to the store and get me a nice head of lettuce," I dropped the stick, took the money, and went.

If she didn't like the lettuce and complained, "Take this back and tell the man I want a *firm* head," I did it. I knew that every leaf of lettuce counted — and the firmer the head, the more leaves it had. Oh, we knew what it was to be poor all right. So no matter how much I wanted to play stickball, I went back with the lettuce. If I didn't, it would make my mother unhappy.

I don't like to make people unhappy. Not my mother, not Lily, not anybody. So when I had my next appointment with Dr. Abel, I had to tell him what Lily told me to tell him.

"My wife said you haven't done very well by me, Dr. Abel, and for me to tell you so."

"Thank you for giving me her message."

"She told me that breaking dishes is better than therapy."

"It's probably cheaper."

"That's what Lily said!"

"You married a very wise woman."

"Do you really think so?"

"Everything you tell me points to that conclusion."

"Then she must be right when things go wrong and she says it's my fault. It's never her fault. She never admits when she's wrong."

"You blame her and she blames you."

"That's it."

"Someone always has to be wrong."

"Only when it's right to be wrong. At least I admit when I'm wrong. If it's my fault, I take the blame. Lily never takes the blame for anything."

"The two of you live in a system of her blame and your fault."

"Oh, sometimes she admits she's wrong. But then I feel guilty. How do you explain that?"

"You always win."

"Win? I always lose."

"When you lose, you win. And when you win, you lose."

"How can anybody live like that? There's no stability."

"There's a lot of stability because it's consistent."

"But I never have any real enjoyment. Why? Why can't I enjoy myself?"

"If you enjoyed yourself, you wouldn't find any pleasure in it."

"Oh, am I glad this tape is running, Dr. Abel. You just contradicted yourself."

"That's not a contradiction. It's an accurate description of your lifestyle."

"Are you suggesting that I actually like to suffer?"

"Most people do. Give me an example of when you suffer."

"Well, just last night, when Lily took a bath and cried because there were no bubbles in the tub because she'd run out of bubble bath. I was disconsolate."

"Because she had no bubbles?"

"Yes. It was my fault. I'd forgotten to remind her to buy another bottle of bubble bath."

"You could have bought it for her."

"Oh, God, don't rub it in. I feel guilty enough. That's why I suffer, because I always have guilt about something."

"It's the second greatest virtue."

"What is?"

"Guilt. If you can't have what you want, even bubbles, guilt is the next best thing."

"Such little things? Why do such little things drive me crazy? Like Lily losing one of my socks in the washing machine. Little things like that are going to break up my marriage!"

"They'll keep it thriving. It isn't orgasms that keep marriages together. It's lost socks that are really important."

"Not to Lily. To her they're nothing but trifles."
He laughed.
"Dr. Abel, why are you laughing?"
"Excuse me. It's a private joke but I'll let you in on it. You see, it's those trifles that make psychiatrists rich."
"You mean I'm not the only one who feels this way?"
"You're not alone."
"Then I guess the whole world is crazy."
"Thank God."
"I beg your pardon, doctor?"
"Never mind, Mr. Flom. Just hang on to your sense of humor."

*I*t isn't easy to keep your sense of humor if you have to ride the New York City subway. I used to think I was suffering from paranoia until I learned that everybody at *Tomorrow* was too. One reporter, Hubie, dreamed up the brilliant idea of playing crazy to ward off would-be muggers. He would always stand, even when seats were available, and twitch and talk to himself.

"Loonies are the only ones safe from muggers," he explained. "I just stand there going yobba yobba yobba and they leave me alone."

I kept wanting to try it but was worried that someone I knew might see me. That prospect outweighed my fear of being mugged.

In the newsroom, on the other hand, being a loony dealing with loonies was no big deal. That was the norm. Every tick of the clock brought another break with reality. It could come in the form of a phone call, a letter, or a barked order from Levin.

Today it started with a phone call from a reader who demanded to talk to the medical editor. Levin told me to take it.

With my tape recorder on and an inconspicuous little bug that enabled me to tape the caller, I said cheerily, "Hello. Can I help you?"

"I hope so. Are you the medical editor?"

"That's right. Who are you?"

"Don't ask my name, please. I'm calling because on the telephone it's private and we don't see each other."

"Okay."

"I keep hearing about oral sex."

"How's that again?"

"Oral sex. Please explain."

"You're putting me on."

"That's oral sex?"

"No, no. I mean, you can't be serious."

"I'm very serious, mister editor. Oral to me has to do with the voice... talking, right? That's oral sex, talking?"

"Oh, shit!"

"What?"

"I said that's not it. Listen, sir, why don't you send in your question and I'll relay it to our research department?"

"I read your paper every week and I know you like to help people. That's why I'm calling."

"We appreciate your interest in our family weekly. So send us a letter, okay?"

"Should I send it to the Oral Sex Department?"

"Oh no, that won't be necessary. Just send it to the paper and I'll see that the right people get it. Thank you for calling."

After hanging up, I started thinking to myself how Lily was going to love hearing about this conversation. At first she'll be shocked, and then she'll giggle embarrassedly and call me a dirty old man. But all the while I'll know she's loving every word. What a great thing to look forward to!

My reverie was interrupted by Desmond, the articles editor at the next desk.

"Sounds like you had a bloody fruitcake on there, eh, Joel? What did he want?"

"He wanted me to explain oral sex to him."

"Oh dear, oh dear, I hope you gave him a mouthful!" he laughed, and I laughed.

I liked Desmond. Dapper, well-mannered, he'd learned the tabloid business on London's Fleet Street and possessed a great British accent that made crud sound classy. Listening to him, it was hard to believe that his was the creative mind responsible for one of the most treasured headlines in tabloid journalism:

NO MONEY FOR TURKEY, MOM ROASTS BABY FOR THANKSGIVING DINNER.

His cultivated speech and manner was a great asset that enabled him to convince people that they were dealing with a distinguished weekly journal. No one knew this better than Levin. In the crunch, he always called upon Desmond to contact celebrated members of Congress, high society or show biz people.

"Everybody, drop whatever you're doing!"

It was Levin, scowling dramatically as he stood tall behind his desk. I could feel the fear rising in my throat. Nobody moved.

"I just heard from the publisher. Our circulation has taken a big drop. We have to come up with a headline that will sell papers, and we have to do it now. Put everything else out of your mind and come up with a lead story. Think big. Think of Elvis, Marilyn, Jackie. Someone whose name will hit the heart and pocketbook of every goddamned supermarket shopper. Now get cracking!"

Elvis, Marilyn, Jackie. After all these years, I couldn't believe they were still good copy. But who was I to argue with the dean of the tabloids? He was schooled in the folklore of the tabloid press where past and present, the living and the dead, are all the same if you can use a memorable name in a sensational headline.

"Well, any ideas?"

Nobody answered. I felt like a dummy. When I saw him approaching my desk, I wanted to crawl under it. What did I know about Elvis, Marilyn or Jackie? Nothing, except what Lily's mother had mentioned because the only things she ever read were tabloids that she found in the incinerator. But it wasn't me who Levin wanted. It was Desmond.

"Hey, Des, did you ever get hold of the guy who claimed Jackie jilted him for JFK?"

"Yes, indeed. I've been after him for years, but he won't talk to me."

Levin seemed inspired. He began to think out loud. In headlines.

"EXCLUSIVE — THE FIRST INTERVIEW WITH THE BEAU JACKIE JILTED FOR JFK!

That would make a dynamite front page."

"But I didn't get the bloody interview."

"I know that. You've been sitting next to Flom so long you've forgotten what the newspaper business is all about. Of course you didn't get the interview. But you got the story and don't even realize it. *Tomorrow* reveals for the first time how he refused to talk about his relationship with Jackie. Right?"

"Righto!"

Levin beamed happily and turned to me. "You see, Flom, this is how we're going to get not one, but two big stories. We make up the first one. Then this old beau of Jackie's calls up to complain. That gives us a chance to wheedle the real story out of him. No matter what he says, we print it. That's called piggy-back journalism, the backbone of the tabloids. See, you learned something today."

I just nodded. I couldn't wait to tell Lily what happened. I had so many wonderful stories to tell her. She loves gossip even if it's only bullshit. Especially if it's bullshit. Come to think of it, that's what makes it interesting!

The THI was breaking records. I was so grateful for having caught an air-conditioned subway train that some primordial impulse began to direct my feet to the neighborhood synagogue to thank God instead of heading for home. But my rational mind took over and turned me in the right direction.

When I reach my apartment, I always like to ring and make Lily come to the door. I like to hear her ask, "Don't you have a key?" Then I say, "Sure, but I didn't want to scare you." It's a regular ritual and it makes Lily furious.

But not this time. She greeted me with a kiss.

Startled, I asked, "What's wrong?"

"My mother's here."

"I knew when you kissed me that something awful had happened."

"Ssshhhh, she's taking a nap."

"Whenever you look at her, she's taking a nap. She gets a good night's sleep at least three times a day."

"That's because she's lonely since my father died."
"My father died too."
"Mine was only 68 when he died. Yours was 73."
"Mine suffered before he died. Yours went fast."
"I'll never kiss you again."
"Why didn't you kiss me because you love me and not because your mother is here?"
"I'm not the demonstrative type."
"Didn't your family kiss one another when they got together?"
"No, they argued."
"Poor Lily. Never mind, I'm going to make you laugh. I've got some great stories to tell you about what went on at the paper today."
"I hope they're clean."

Before I could answer, we were interrupted by a loud cry from the bedroom. "Is that you, Joel?" Lily's mother was up from her nap. I went in.
"Hi. It's good to see you. How are you feeling?"
"I'm all washed out."
"Well, you had a nice nap."
"I never closed my eyes. I just laid there."
"Look, I'm wearing your new tie. How does it look?"
"Very nice. I gave you one just like it. Why don't you ever wear it?"
"I'm wearing it now."
"I thought so. You're just coming home from work? How's the job?"
"Terrible."

"That's all right. You're making money. That's what counts."

Lily came charging into the bedroom, chattering excitedly, "Mom, I talked to cousin Minnie this morning. She said Abe is having trouble with his eyes. He may go blind."

"Oh my, now she'll have to lead him around everywhere."

"I also heard from Uncle Louie and Aunt Bella. They invited Joel and me to their house for dinner."

"Good. Make sure you eat plenty."

These were Lily's most interesting relatives. Louie was her uncle by marriage, a true gourmet cook who often entertained such culinary luminaries as Craig Claiborne and Pierre Franey at his 200-year-old house in Connecticut. I always looked forward to dinner there because the food was sure to be offbeat and memorable. Lily's mother had no interest in anything more exotic than stuffed derma and lox with eggs and onions.

"It will be a very special meal," Lily told her. "Uncle Louie said we'll start off with eels in green sauce."

"Pfeh!"

"And then he's going to serve braised pigeons."

"Pfeh!"

"Pigeons are very hard to find."

"Tell him to come to my apartment. They're at my window day and night making *dreck*."

"These aren't the same kinds of pigeons," I explained.

"You're getting just like him," she said. "I'm going to the kitchen and have a nice cup of tea for my condition."

As we watched her shuffle off, Lily said, "She's getting so weak she can hardly get around any more."

"She doesn't look weak to me."

"No, only *your* mother is weak!"

"Listen, Lily, the difference between your mother and mine is that mine pretends she *isn't* weak and yours pretends she *is*."

"Spoken like a true loyal son!"

"Please, enough!"

"Sure, now you'll avoid everything by going into the kids' room, closing the door, lighting up a cigarette and taking a drink."

"Maybe I will and maybe I won't."

"You smoke too much and drink too much. You spend all that money smoking, drinking, and seeing a shrink. What a waste!"

"Can't you be a little kinder, Lily?"

"Whatever I say is for your own good. I don't want you to die and leave me a widow. What would I do? What would the children do?"

"They don't need me anymore. David is 23 and in a prestigious medical school. Billy is almost 22 and in a prestigious law school. I've done everything a Jewish father can do."

"You're also a Jewish husband. I'm going to give you the biggest funeral of your life so my friends will think you left me well provided for."

She stormed off, leaving me to feel like a total failure.

That last conversation with Lily was unnerving. We've had our ups and downs before but this time she seemed like a different person. I was in a terrible state by the time of my next session with Dr. Abel. I came right to the point.

"Lily has changed."

"Congratulations."

"No, no, not for the better. She's a different person. I'm beginning to think that she is really *two* women."

"Your cup runneth over."

"I wish you'd share my concern."

"Believe me, Mr. Flom, I do share your concern, but not your problem."

"I need sympathy."

"I'm a psychiatrist, not a rabbi. What has Lily done to make you slump back in the chair like that, your face all scrunched up, your voice so filled with anguish?"

"Well, I hate to say this, but I'm convinced she has two distinct personalities. One is tender and loving, that's the Lily I married. The other is mean and unforgiving, that's the one who causes me heartache."

"So you believe you married the first one, not the second."

"Exactly. That's the one I fell in love with, the real Lily. But when she isn't herself, her real self, I don't like her."

"Maybe that's when you like her more."

"When she's mean to me?"

"That's your reward."

"My punishment, not my reward."

"With you it's all the same, punishment and rewards, winning and losing, success and failure..."

"That's it! She practically called me a failure."

"That's her way of calling you a success. You two have so much in common it's a match made in heaven."

"You mean there really aren't two Lilys, only one?"

"One alone, just like always. Sometimes she expresses herself tenderly and other times she doesn't, that's all."

"How come when I married her I only saw the tender side?"

"That's all you wanted to see. It's not unusual in marriages."

"I understand what you're saying, Dr. Abel. But when she criticizes me, it hurts, even though I know she's doing it for my own good."

"Like what, for instance?"

"Well, take my drinking. She knows it's bad for my health."

"How much do you drink?"

"Oh, I like to take a shot now and then. But if she catches me, oh boy!"

"What does she say when she catches you?"

"Put down that glass! Don't drink so much! You'll become a drunk!"

"How do you answer her?"

"At first I get angry. Then I realize she's looking after my best interests and so I say something like, 'Lily, it's your job to look after me and see that I don't drink too much.'"

"You want her to keep nagging."

"Who said anything about nagging? I said she should look after me."

"Put down that glass! Don't drink so much! What is that?"

I was stunned by that revelation. After several seconds of expensive silence, I said, "Maybe so, doctor, but sometimes my head hurts after I take a drink and Lily has to remind me that I'm becoming an alcoholic."

"One or two drinks won't make your head hurt, Mr. Flom. The pain comes from the battles going on inside your head. Life is war to you and you're always at the front like a good soldier. Your problem is combat fatigue, not alcoholism."

"Well, I suppose it's because I'm Jewish."

"Oh?"

"I mean the drinking part. You know that Jewish people can't drink. They're not like other people. Their internal plumbing is different. That's why they're always taking *Maalox* or *Mylanta*."

"So you consider a drinking problem a Jewish problem."

"Most likely. Jewish men have so many responsibilities. I know because I have them too. I have to worry about Lily, my kids, my mother, my mother-in-law. There's hardly time in the day to take care of my job."

"Looking after everybody, that's your *real* job."

"They make it my job. They all put these responsibilities on my back, especially Lily."

"Now you're talking like a Jewish husband."

"I'm not sure I understand."

"A Jewish husband is a donkey. He allows others to load him down with responsibilities and then he blames them for doing so."

"Ah, so then he becomes angry with himself."

"No. The peculiar thing is that he likes it. We'll have to stop now, Mr. Flom. You can turn off the tape recorder."

*I*f it wasn't Lily, it was the THI that undid the benefits of my treatment. Once again New York was broiling. On my way to the office, I thought I'd pass out from the anxiety brought on by blazing heat and drenching humidity. I couldn't wait to get out of the street and into the air-conditioned office. But when I got there on this awful oppressive morning, the newsroom was far from being cool and comforting.

I looked down the line of desks. Sure enough, there was a window open where one of the reporters, a southerner from Alabama, sat. His idea of cool was 75 degrees. Somehow Levin must have been too absorbed to notice and nobody else had dared to speak up.

After going to my desk and switching on the tape recorder, I got up my courage and went directly to Levin. "Excuse me, but we're having a meeting with the publisher today, aren't we?"

"Yeah, what about it?"

"Well, the publisher hates the heat and it's pretty sticky in here. I notice there's a window open letting in the hot air."

He looked up and screamed, "'Bama! Shut that fucking window! What's the big idea? You know our publisher's coming here for a meeting and he likes it cool."

"Well, ah just thought we oughtta have a little fresh air in here."

"We don't need fresh air. We need fresh ideas. Now shut the fucking window!"

'Bama slammed it down, then made a face and reached into his desk drawer for a sweater. I'd won my first battle of the day. Now I was ready to tackle the pile of mail on my desk.

The first letter I picked up was addressed to the medical editor by a man who wrote. "I'm very fat and have a sex problem. Is there any way I can make my body smaller or my penis larger?"

I put it in my pocket to show to Lily, then picked up another letter sent to the attention of the science editor. It was from a woman who claimed to have a boyfriend who was born on the moon. Her descriptions of moon life were spellbinding and topped off by this final paragraph, "Those LEM modules our astronauts left there are being used as jungle gyms by the moon children. It would make a nice story for *Tomorrow*. How much do you pay?"

Lily & Joel

I passed it on to the photo editor with a note to have the woman send pictures to back up the story. It was early but my rational mind was already beginning to go.

"Hubie!"

It was Levin. When he had something to say, he didn't approach a reporter personally. He just raised his voice. This time his target was Hubie, the one who talks to himself while riding the subway.

"I'm reading your story about this week's TV cover girl that the stringer phoned in to you."

"Is it okay?"

"You wrote that she has a cocksure lover. Damn it, we can't say that in a family newspaper!"

"That's what the stringer called him."

"Well, you should know better. I'm changing it to read 'she has an aggressive lover.' Use your wits next time."

Levin then turned his attention to Desmond. "You did the Bruce Willis story we ran two weeks ago, didn't you?"

"Yes, indeed," acknowledged Desmond cheerily.

"Well, if you want to read it again, take a look at this week's *People* magazine. Am I mistaken or do they have our exact quotes on the cover?"

Desmond's eyes flashed. "If they do, they stole them from us. What a bloody breach of ethics."

"Or maybe they got them from the same guy you did."

"Impossible. I made up those quotes!"

Desmond was shattered. I started to commiserate with him when I became aware that a sudden hush had fallen over the newsroom. I looked up. My old college chum, the publisher, had quietly made his entrance.

Impulsively, I raced over to him, gave him the old college handshake, and greeted him by his first name, Harold. Nobody else, including Levin, dared to call him anything except Mr. Drucker. He always gave me a big hello. This made Levin insanely jealous. I loved it.

"How are you, Joel? How is Lily? How's everything going?"

Three questions. Always. He had this peculiar habit of asking questions in threes. One more and he'd sound like he was conducting a seder.

"We're all fine, Harold. Everything is fine. How about you and your wife?"

"Wonderful. The divorce is proceeding nicely."

Our small talk was interrupted by an envious Levin. "I know your time is valuable, Mr. Drucker, so I thought you'd like to get the meeting started. Is there any special problem we should take up first?"

"We need some real blockbuster stories to hype the circulation. Don't you agree? What do you think? Am I right?"

"Absolutely, Mr. Drucker."

"Good. I have an idea."

Then he turned to me and said earnestly, "Joel, we've been getting a lot of mail about our miracle stories and I'd like to do more of them. Could you do that? Would you handle that for me? Can you get your professional contacts to give us first crack at good miracle stories?"

"Professional miracles?"

"That's it. You know, miracle drugs, miracle diets, miracle births, all kinds of spectacular breakthroughs. That word 'miracle' in a headline always sends our circulation soaring. But I'd like you to use your good professional sources to upgrade the quality of these stories. What we need are more important miracles."

It was an awesome assignment.

"Well, Harold, I'll do my best. But I have to be able to reassure my contacts that they'll be quoted accurately."

"Naturally, Joel. You'll be in complete charge of all miracle copy. Levin will see to it. Right? Okay? Agreed?"

"Right," said Levin reluctantly.

The look he gave me made it clear that he wasn't going to make my job easy. So what? I had the publisher on my side. And Dr. Abel. And Lily.

And Lily?

I was putting a fresh cassette in my tape recorder and hiding it under the bed while Lily was having her bath. By the time she came out, I was under the covers. Before she joined me, she reached into her handbag and took out some letters.

"Here, Joel, I forgot to give you the mail."

I was furious.

"Don't look at me like that," she said. "There's nothing important here."

"Maybe not to you."

I glanced through the mail. Bills, junk, more bills.

"Hey, wait, here's a letter from David's medical school."

"It's not for you, it's for David. Don't open it."

"It might be important."

"Forward it to him. He'll get it."

Before she could say another word, I tore open the envelope.

"Wow! It's from the dean. David was elected to the medical honor society!"

"Why are you so glad? It didn't happen to you."

"We'll call him right now and give him the good news."

"No, we won't. Just put that letter back in the envelope and mark it 'Opened By Mistake.' He'll get it in a few days."

"Good news like this can't wait. He'll be so happy, so impressed, to know how highly he's regarded."

"David doesn't care what people think."

"Honors are important. They pave the way to success."

"You've had more honors than I have roaches in the kitchen. So how come you're still struggling?"

"Being a writer is not like being a doctor."

"Now you sound like my mother."

"I don't understand you, Lily. Here is something to be proud of and you make so little of it. The poor kid is working his ass off as a busboy at the fabulous Concord Resort in the Catskills. The least we can do is give him this bit of pleasure."

"Big tips will give him more pleasure. Don't feel so sorry for him, Joel. He's not having such a bad time and he's making a lot of money for himself."

"Not for himself. For me. Because I can't afford to pay his way through medical school like other fathers."

Life, Love and AudioTapes

"You're a real Jewish father. Why can't you be like the Rockefellers? Their kids worked and they weren't ashamed."

"I'm not ashamed. I just feel that I've let him down. Billy too."

"Why do you mention Billy? You mention one son, so you have to mention the other, is that it?"

"No, that's not it."

"Then why did you mention Billy when you were talking about David?"

"Because I let him down too. What is he doing this summer? Having a good time? No, he's working his ass off in Boston to help make it through law school."

"Yes, Joel, and when he gets his law degree, he'll be making more money than you are. And when David becomes a doctor, he'll be making more money than the both of you."

"That's not fair. Even though I may not make a lot of money, I'm a somebody."

"Between assignments, you're not anything. You're just in the house."

"There you go again. One minute you compliment me about my honors, the next minute you berate me. I never know what to expect from you."

"That will keep you from ever taking me for granted."

"If it wasn't for you, I'd never have gone to work at *Tomorrow*. I hate the job. It's more than I can handle."

55

Lily & Joel

"That isn't true. You're so smart you can handle anything."

That was the Lily I'd married. Adoring, grateful, a true wife. I was deeply touched.

"Do you really mean that?"

"If I didn't mean it, would I say it?"

"Well, there are times you say things you don't mean."

"It all depends on what I'm saying."

We were interrupted by the telephone. I tensed up.

"Don't be nervous. It's only one of the kids. You know they call after eleven when it's cheaper."

"Hurry up, get the phone. It might be my mother."

"If it's important, she'll call again."

"If she can!"

I hated to miss phone calls, but I also hated to answer the phone. You never know what you'll hear. None of this bothered Lily. And it bothered me that it didn't bother her.

The phone kept ringing and she finally picked it up. I was relieved to hear her talking to Billy and sounding very calm. Usually, she talked interminably but this time she hung up within seconds.

"Billy just wanted us to know that he and Dawn are driving in this weekend."

"Did he say why?"

"No, just that they don't have anything special to do in Boston."

I was suspicious. Billy met Dawn at law school and fell for her at once. Lily and I did too, when we met her on a visit to the school. She was pretty and she was smart. But one thing troubled Lily. Her first name.

"Dawn. That's a name for a Jewish girl?"

Her last name, Berman, was more reasonable, or so we thought, until Billy reminded us proudly that it was Burman... spelled with a "u", which seemed to him a mark of distinction. Obviously, her family had a thing about being Jewish, which didn't sit so well with Lily. I had told her to relax, their relationship wasn't serious yet. Now I was beginning to have second thoughts about that.

"I have a feeling, Lily, that they're coming here to talk to us about getting married."

"Don't be ridiculous! He's only a baby."

"He's going to be twenty-two."

"They have two more years to go to finish law school!"

"They've been living together."

"Well? So why the big rush to get married?"

"Maybe Dawn's mother is pressing her. She may not be as broad-minded as you."

"Few women are."

"If it was your daughter, not your son, you might feel the same way."

"Not I. My feelings are purely bisexual."

"Billy says her parents are great people and they like him very much."

57

"Why not? He's a good catch."

"He isn't rich like Dawn."

"All the more reason they don't need a rich son-in-law. Where are they going to get a boy like Billy? Handsome, brilliant, clean-cut, and from a good family. A brother who'll be a doctor, a father a famous author, and a mother a New York City School Volunteer."

"Are you going to tell them that?"

"I don't have to. They already know it. And I'm in no hurry to meet her family. It's all too rush-rush. The kids should wait until they finish law school. And that's my last word on the subject. I don't want to talk about it any more. Let's drop it!"

That's how Lily resolved all her problems. She ignored them.

They couldn't have picked a worse weekend to visit us. Thunder, lightning, heavy rain. And no let-up in the heat and humidity. With every rise in the THI, I thought to myself, oh God, there goes another brain cell!

Anyone who leaves an air-conditioned apartment on a day like this must be crazy. And driving in this weather is really hazardous, as I kept telling Lily.

"Do me a favor. Call Billy and tell him and Dawn not to drive in today."

"It's too late. They're already on their way."

"They could have taken the train. This is no day to drive."

"Go into the bedroom and take a nap."

"How can you be so calm?"

"Somebody has to be."

The telephone rang.

"The phone!"

Lily & Joel

"All right, all right. I'll get it, Joel... It's your mother. She's on the alert. Here."

I took the phone.

"Hi, Mom."

"Is Billy driving in this weather?"

"Yes, but don't worry."

"I can't even see out the window, it's raining so hard. I don't think he should drive."

"He'll be here very soon. Stop worrying."

"Aren't you worried?"

"No, I never worry," I lied.

"Well, you're very peculiar."

The longer she talked, the more nervous I became.

"Listen, Mom, I'll call you the minute he gets here. Everything will be all right."

"I can't understand him driving in this weather."

"He'll be all right, Mom, he'll be all right!"

"Don't get so excited, Joel. You're very excitable."

"I know, I know."

"My goodness. Try to get hold of yourself."

"Let me get off the phone, Mom, please. I'm expecting another call."

"I have to ask you something."

Oh, no. I was filled with dread. "What's the matter?"

"Well, I was listening to the radio and heard some cancer specialists talking about *Lomotil*. Isn't that the medicine I'm taking for my diarrhea?"

"Yes, but they must have been talking about *Laetrile*, not *Lomotil*."

"They said it was made from apricot pits."

"That's right."

"Does that mean I shouldn't drink apricot juice any more?"

"No, no, it's perfectly safe."

"It's the first time I heard that apricot pits were cancerous. You know I drink it for my potassium."

"I know. It's okay, Mom. Keep drinking it."

"You're sure?"

"I'm absolutely, positively sure. Now please let me get off the phone!"

I was so agitated I hung up without waiting for an answer.

"I was wondering when she'd call," said Lily, smirking.

I headed for the table where we kept the Scotch. But Lily was vigilant.

"No drinks, Joel! The kids are coming."

That didn't stop me. The doorbell did. In came the kids, wet but unharmed.

"Well, we made it," said Billy, laughing and looking straight at me as if he knew what I was thinking.

"I knew you would," I lied. "How was the driving?"

"Just awful," said Dawn. "I had to keep telling him to slow down."

"Oh, she's just being dramatic," he scoffed.

While Lily gave them hugs and kisses, I excused myself and went into the bedroom to phone my mother and reassure her that the kids had arrived safe and sound.

"See," my mother said, "I told you there was nothing to worry about."

It was hopeless. Everything was hopeless. I wished I had a drink but the drinks were in the living room, so I gulped down a *Valium* instead. When I came back in, they were all talking together, animatedly. Something was afoot. Lily seemed very uncomfortable.

"Billy has something to tell you," she said, quietly.

"Good news, I hope."

"We think so," said Billy. "Dawn and I want to get married."

"Married? Great! When you both graduate, right?"

"That's two years away, Dad."

"You're telling me? Don't you think I keep track of your progress? You'll both graduate in May and you'll have a June wedding. Right, Dawn?"

"No, we'd like to marry when we're through with our summer jobs this August."

I felt intimidated. I found myself thinking this girl would be a great lawyer. Lily seemed to be gathering herself together for a major confrontation but was obviously holding back. She turned to me instead.

"Joel, don't you think they'd be better off waiting until they get their law degrees?"

Billy answered before I could agree with her.

"Why should we wait, Mom?"

"Because you're both still students," she said, quite logically and persuasively, I thought. Billy didn't.

"But we've been living together for a year."

"I know, darling, but you've been in a protected environment, not in the real world."

"I'm working for a labor union this summer and Dawn's working for the Legal Aid Society. What's unreal about that?"

"Tell them, Lily," I said, encouragingly.

She chose her words with care, thinking harder than I'd ever seen her think before.

"You know how fond we are of you, Dawn, and we're delighted that you and Billy are in love and want to be married. But neither of you are on your own yet. You're still being supported, isn't that right, Billy?"

"Well, you'll still help me with my tuition — and with loans, my savings, and summer jobs, it won't be any different whether we're married or just living together."

"That's not the point. Dawn has had advantages that you don't have. And it isn't fair to her for you to marry until you become a lawyer and have a good job so you can give her all the things she's used to having."

Dawn looked Lily straight in the eye. "You mean because my father's rich it's a problem?"

"Of course not! Money isn't everything."

"You just said it is."

Billy came to the rescue. "Look, Mom, we've talked all about this. It's not a problem."

"Did you discuss this with your mother, Dawn, I mean about getting married... now?"

"Oh, sure. She's all for it. She's crazy about Billy. So is my father. You're the only ones who want us to postpone the marriage."

Lily was decidedly uncomfortable. So was I. We were losing.

Billy broke the tension with a laugh. "They know I'm not marrying Dawn for her money."

"Naturally! We all know that. That's why we're talking like human beings. We want to be fair to Dawn. And the fact is that you do come from different backgrounds."

"We're all Jewish," he said.

"Yes," chirped Dawn. "My mother was glad to hear I was going with a Jewish boy."

"Oh? Is your mother very religious?"

"Not really. She's just Jewish."

"Like us. That's nice."

Billy was shaking his head incredulously. "I think this whole conversation is ridiculous. We're in love and want to get married, that's all there is to it."

"Of course, darling. Your father and I just want to be sure you're doing the right thing."

"And at the right time," I added.

But I knew all along it was going to be a lost cause. Billy always got his way. Still, I couldn't see the need for haste. Marriage is no picnic. The thought of divorce had crossed my mind many times. But, as Dr. Abel told me, Jewish couples with children don't divorce so quickly. It's the old story about couples who never got along but didn't get divorced until they were in their eighties and the children were dead.

I felt sure that Billy and Dawn would be good for each other because their personalities seemed to mesh. What troubled me was his having a rich father-in-law.

Would that make me a second-class father?

I brooded over this, unable to resolve my conflicting emotions without help from Dr. Abel. Making things worse was the fact that there was no break in the sweltering THI. When the time finally came for my appointment, my *angst* knew no bounds.

"I have a terrible feeling, doctor, that I've done very badly by my children."

"In what way?"

"I'm not a first-class father. I'm only a second-class father."

"This is something new, Mr. Flom. Why do you consider yourself a second-class father?"

"Because my younger son, Billy, wants to marry a girl whose father is rich, rich, rich!"

"*Mazeltov!*"

"It's an uneven match, except that this man isn't a professional person like me."

"He's just rich."

"One of the biggest garage kings in the country. He started out with one little parking lot. Now he owns hundreds. Can you imagine a man making so much money on parking lots?"

"He must be a good businessman."

"Precisely. That's what bothers me."

"You prefer him to be a bad businessman?"

"I just don't understand how anyone who went to college doesn't use his education."

"He uses it to make money."

"You sound like my father. He used to say to me, 'Your best friend is your dollar.' No, I have it wrong. What he said was 'Your *only* friend is your dollar.'"

"That's even better."

"It's because we were poor. I got so many clothes from the bargain basement I thought *Irregulars* was a brand name like *Wranglers* or *Levis*."

"That was long ago. You aren't poor now."

"But I feel poor."

"You only feel the way you think you should feel. It's part of your heritage."

"Maybe I take after my father. He set very high standards for me like I do for my kids. When I was still in high school, I sold my first story to a magazine for $25 and felt very proud of myself. But when my father heard what I was paid, he said, 'That's all?.'"

"How did that make you feel?"

"How do you think? Worthless."

"Worthless. Compared to what your father thought you were worth."

"Of course."

"So now you compare yourself unfavorably to your son's intended father-in-law because he's the kind of man you think your father would be proud of."

"Oh, would he! I should have listened to my father."

"You did listen."

"Then why aren't I rich?"

"Because you didn't hear what he said."

"You told me I did listen."

"You listened but you didn't hear. There's a world of difference between the two. Your father was trying to tell you that you had a superior mind but he expressed your worth in terms of money because he didn't have any. If he were alive today, he'd be prouder of you for being a writer than a parking lot tycoon."

I was too overcome to speak. Finally, I said, "Dr. Abel, you've lifted my spirits more than I can put into words."

"Congratulations. You've had a catharsis."

"I'm on a cloud. What you just told me is something I'd like to believe I knew all the time, but I didn't."

"Let me reveal a professional secret, Mr. Flom. You really did know. I never tell anybody anything they don't already know. Unfortunately for them, but fortunately for me, they don't know they know it until I tell them."

My self-esteem was zooming higher than the THI.

*I*f anyone can tolerate the heat and humidity better than Lily, it's her mother. The THI can reach a record breaking 95 and she'll complain, "It's cold." When I asked her doctor why, his answer was, "She isn't really cold, she's old."

Such smart-ass explanations never satisfied me. I have to get a proper medical diagnosis. Lily says this is why no doctor except Dr. Abel likes to treat me. I ask too many questions.

Lily's mother never asks questions. She issues directives: "Give me something to sleep"; "Do something for my appetite"; "Look at my feet."

When I arrived home from work, there she was, at my apartment and waiting for me.

"It's about time you got here. Where have you been?"

"Working," I said, suppressing my rage. "Here's an advance copy of *Tomorrow*. It won't be on the stands until next week."

Lily & Joel

"That's a very nice paper. I like it even better than the *Enquirer*."

"You'll like the story in this issue about the life of the Duchess of Windsor. You know, the one who was married to the Duke."

"That bum."

"Why do you call him a bum?"

"He was nothing but a runaround."

"She led a pretty fast life herself."

"One thing I'll say for him. He was very good to her. He gave her anything she wanted. Some man!"

I had the feeling that remark was directed at me. My self-esteem would have plunged to the lower depths if it hadn't been buoyed up by my earlier session with Dr. Abel. So I ignored it and changed the subject.

"You're looking well."

"I look well to you?"

"Yes. How do you feel."

"I don't know if I'll be around much longer."

Lily came to the rescue, handing me a letter. "Here, Joel. You got an invitation to a big party from your old friend, Murray."

"He's no friend. He's probably promoting some half-assed gadget or other and wants me to give him some free publicity."

"Never mind," said Lily's mother. "Don't miss out. Go with Lily and have a good time."

"He's a promoter," Lily explained, "and he's worth millions."

"He treats people like dirt unless they can do something for him," I said, "and that makes me mad."

Lily's mother gave me a piercing look. "You don't get mad at a man with that kind of money."

"He can't be so bad," said Lily. "When he got divorced, the court awarded him custody of their little girl."

"His wife must be a prostitute," said Lily's mother.

"No, she has a big job with an advertising agency and travels a lot. That's why she didn't get custody. Sometimes I envy her."

"You envy her?"

"Sure, Ma. Now that David and Billy are grown up, I'd like to get a job."

"Oh, go on! What's the matter with you?"

"This is a different world, Ma. Women can do things."

"You're doing plenty."

"Even cousin Flo is looking for a part-time job."

"That dumbbell. You compare yourself to her?"

"She isn't even well and she wants to work. She has a spastic colon."

"She's like an ox. She's lucky she got herself a klutz like Sidney to shlep her around from one doctor to another."

"He must love her very deeply," I said.

"He never was much. If she'd take a cup of tea and a good hot bath, she wouldn't need doctors. I think I'll go into the bedroom now and take a little nap. You two do whatever you want."

After she closed the door behind her, I looked at Lily and said just loud enough for the tape to pick it up, "I thought she has trouble sleeping."

"If you're looking for an argument, you'll get one."

"How come she didn't say anything about Billy and Dawn wanting to get married? Didn't you tell her?"

"Why should I tell her? It isn't definite."

"It will be soon."

"When I say it will be, that's when it will be. Now please excuse me while I go and put an extra blanket on my mother for her little nap."

"I suppose she's going to stay overnight."

"So?"

"So I figure that between this little nap and a full night's sleep she'll have slept at least sixteen hours. And she'll still complain that she can't sleep."

"That's her privilege."

"Why?"

"Because she's my mother."

Even the Old Testament would have a good word for Lily.

The miracles recounted in the Old Testament had nothing on the miracles headlined by *Tomorrow*. I was sweating out this project that my friend, the publisher, had assigned me, and Levin never let me forget it.

No matter how early I arrived at the office, the phones were ringing and Levin was hollering, "Grab that phone, Flom! It might be a miracle story."

He made me so anxious I hardly had time to set up my tape recorder before picking up the phone to.ask, "This is *Tomorrow*. Who's calling?"

"I'm Sammy Groshinski from the old age home. You called me yesterday late?"

"Oh, yes, Mr. Groshinski. We heard that you'll soon be celebrating your one-hundredth birthday."

"Right, a hundred."

"That's wonderful. We'd like to do a story about you."

"What kind of story?"

"An inspirational story, about the miracle of growing old."

"That's a miracle by you?"

"Well, it is a wonderful thing for someone to grow older and still be in the prime of life, in a way of speaking. So your life could be a great inspiration to our readers."

"If you say so."

"Fine, fine. Now tell me, Mr. Groshinski, what is your secret of staying young?"

"Who's young? I'm going to be a hundred."

"Yes, and for that reason *Tomorrow* wants to wish you a very happy birthday. How does it feel to be 100?"

"I wish I was dead."

It was too much. I hung up, feeling absolutely mortified, and found Levin breathing down my neck.

"You blew that story, didn't you, Flom?" he sneered.

"There was no story, Levin. This guy would rather be dead than be a hundred years old."

"A good reporter would change his mind. I want to remind you that we lock up today and we have to headline a miracle story on the front page. I'm going to use your magic toenail story for the lead headline."

"What magic toenail story?"

"Here, I'll read you the headline."

He read it aloud.

"IT'S MAGIC... MIRACLE LOTION CURES INGROWN TOENAILS WHILE YOU SLEEP!"

I couldn't believe it.

"It's not a magical lotion. It's just an advanced form of mercurochrome that helps treat ingrown toenails."

"It kills pain, doesn't it?"

"Well, it helps."

"We know from our mail that millions of our readers suffer from ingrown toenails. They'd love to hear about a new treatment for this painful problem."

"All right, then let's just say that. Change the word 'cures' to 'treats.' That'll do it."

"You still don't understand, do you, Flom? Our readers don't want to be treated. They want to be cured. That's why it's a miracle. And that's what you're supposed to be doing, coming up with miracles to boost our circulation."

"But the publisher wants to upgrade the paper by giving it more credibility."

"What's more credible than a miracle? Who except God can question a miracle? Here you've got a pretty good one and you want to kill it."

"I just want it to be believable."

"When we print it, it will be believable. I keep telling you, Flom, that we are not a high-brow publication. We speak the language of the people."

"Maybe you should read the headline to the publisher first."

"I already have. He loves it. Now you don't want to spoil his day by changing it, do you? After all, you're his buddy."

He strutted off, smirking. He had me by the balls and he knew it. What hurt even more was the realization that my old college chum, the publisher, agreed with him.

*L*evin's brand of journalism would not appeal to David, my son the future doctor. His moral principles were so high that he intended to make house calls regularly when he completed his medical education.

"I hope he won't think less of me for going along with such deviousness," I confided to Lily.

"Don't worry about what your children think of you. It's what you think of them that counts."

"You know, I just remembered. David will be twenty four next week. Let's go up to the Concord for the weekend and wish him a happy birthday in person. We'll have a good time."

"You're just looking for an excuse to drink and flirt."

"I have never loved anyone but you, and you know it. I don't flirt."

"You would if you had half a chance."

"If we go, we won't have to see your mother or mine for a whole weekend."

A satisfied smile crossed her face.

"But we'll have to get him a present," I reminded her.

"That custom is passé, Joel. I don't believe in giving presents to children. I should get a present for having them."

"Nobody gave me a present when I turned fifty this year, and I'm a father and a husband."

"But not in that order."

"You make too little of birthdays, of everything, Lily."

"And you make too much."

"I'm a half-century old."

"Then act your age. Now come on, Joel, if you want to go, let's start packing."

While Lily got our things together, I sneaked the tape recorder under the driver's seat of the old Chevy and turned on the automatic gizmo that would start it recording at the sound of a voice. But nothing of import was said during our drive, only my complaints about the broken air-conditioner in the car, and Lily's complaints about my complaints.

It was a great relief to get out of the car and into our air-conditioned room. Lily couldn't understand why I insisted on wearing a jacket. I told her that I felt more comfortable being properly dressed. It was a lie. I just had to wear it to conceal the tape recorder in one of its deep pockets.

David had managed to switch his hours around so that he could spend some time with us. He looked fine, but it hurt me to know that he had to work like a peon as a busboy at this fancy resort while the guests who were not his equals were living it up day and night.

"Are you working hard, David?" I asked him.

"Yeah, Dad, but I'm making lots of money."

Money! The word went through me like a knife.

"That's great," said Lily. "Are you learning anything?"

"Well, I'm learning how much people can eat, Mom. I've never seen anything like it. There isn't an anorectic in the joint. You should see how they eat!"

"They want their money's worth, darling."

"Here's a story you can use in *Tomorrow*, Dad. I had a table with a woman and her grandchild. The kid was about six years old and weighed at least a hundred pounds. But the grandmother kept begging the kid to eat extra helpings of everything and the kid refused. So she took some lox and rubbed it over the kid's lips to get his juices flowing so he could eat more. And he did!"

"That's a great story," I said, laughing. "But this is a special occasion. Almost... because we're a little early. Nevertheless, David, happy birthday."

"Thanks, Dad."

"And congratulations on making the honor society at medical school. You've made your mother and me very proud."

"I didn't expect anything less from you," said Lily.

David gave her a big hug and then turned to me, saying, "Hey, Dad, thanks for sending me that last issue of *Tomorrow*. Do you really make up all that stuff?"

"We call it embroidery, which is a polite term for enlarging on the facts," I said, wincing.

"Fantastic. But how do you get this psychologist who writes for the paper to say all those crazy things?"

"Oh, he's a trained seal. We feed him answers the way a trainer feeds fish to a seal in a circus. We have reporters on the staff who know exactly how to do this."

"I can't believe it!"

"It's a real talent. One reporter, Hubie, is an expert. He'll call up this Doctor So-and-So and ask him, 'Is getting phone calls really bad for the heart?' And the doc will mumble something like 'I'll have to think about it.' But Hubie won't give him a chance to think. He'll say, 'I guess it could be a strain on the heart, hearing the phone ring, wondering who's calling, whether it's bad news. Couldn't that be stressful?' And the doc will say, 'Oh, yes, that could be very stressful.' And Hubie will press on, 'Maybe even make his heart palpitate?' And the doc will say, 'It could happen.' That's how it works. The doc eats up Hubie's words like a trained seal eats fish. And then Hubie turns the doc's words into quotes and the doc is happy so long as he gets his check promptly."

David just shook his head in disbelief. I thought to myself, he'll make ten house calls to earn what the trained seal earns with one phone call.

"We have more important things to talk about," said Lily. "We have news for you, David. Your brother wants to marry Dawn."

"Does that surprise you, Mom?"

"They don't want to wait until they graduate."

"What's going to happen when they graduate?"

"Don't be a smart-aleck."

"But, Mom, he's old enough to make his own decisions. Don't you agree, Dad?"

"Of course," I said, too promptly.

"Are you going against me, Joel?"

"Listen, Lily, if David isn't upset, there must be a reason. After all, he's studying to be a doctor and knows what he's talking about. He made the honor society."

"What does the honor society have to do with it, Dad?"

"David's right," snapped Lily. "You and your honor societies! That's all that impresses you, Joel."

David tried to calm things down. "Listen, both of you are making too much of this. If Billy and Dawn want to get married before they graduate from law school, that's their business. You've done your job."

Done? Suddenly, I felt a lot older than fifty. Lily said nothing, but there was fire in her eyes. It was plain that David was not going to have the last word on this very sore subject.

So, why should things be different for David? I've known Lily longer than he has and I never get the last word. She's so unpredictable I can rarely fathom her next move. It makes life interesting but keeps me on tenterhooks. Only with Dr. Abel do I always know where I stand.

The one thing that distinguishes analysts from other doctors is stability. Every appointment is timed precisely. You never have to wait. If you're scheduled for 12:30, that's when you go in. And you know that you'll be out at 1:15 on the dot. Such precision makes it more convenient to have a neurosis than a lump, a spasm, or a zits.

This time I was so eager to unburden myself that I began babbling even before I sat down. "I'm very depressed today, doctor. I don't think I've ever felt so rotten."

"You look reasonably healthy to me."

"Looks can be deceiving, they say."

"Who are they?"

"Everyone. Even Freud said so."

"Where did he say that?"

"It's the very heart of his theory. Only the unconscious represents one's true face to the world."

"Mr. Flom, if you want to spend your time giving me lessons in psychiatry, that's all right with me. It's your money."

"I'm sorry if I've offended you."

"You can offend me all you like as long as you pay your bills on time."

"You sound like Lily!"

He laughed. At first I was annoyed. Then I found myself laughing too.

"You see, Mr. Flom, how quickly you can get rid of your troubles? Just laugh them away."

"Well, I suppose I do have a bit of a tendency to exaggerate my worries but, believe me, they're very real. I don't let them interfere with my work though. In fact, the publisher has made me editor-in-charge-of-miracles and I'm doing a very good job."

"That's only a temporary job."

"Just for the summer, you mean?"

"No. I mean it's only temporary as compared to your full-time job. Worrying. That's your real job."

"You can't be serious."

"I'm always serious, Mr. Flom, even when I laugh."

"And just what worries occupy so much of my attention?"

"Need I enumerate them? Okay. You worry about Lily, your mother, your mother-in-law, your children, your son's future father-in-law, your grandmother..."

"Now, wait, she's dead a long time."

"That doesn't stop you from worrying about her."

I was beside myself. "Why why why? Why can't I have peace? There's no reason why I shouldn't have peace."

"There is a reason."

"What's the reason?"

"You have *yentas* in your head. They're all up there yapping at you... the living, the dead, it makes no difference."

"Then my worries aren't real?"

"Whatever's in your head is real to you."

"Why is this happening?"

"To put it simply, because you keep going back to your roots."

"You mean that my background still influences my thinking, even though I know better?"

"You don't know better."

"What you're telling me is that I can't break away from my Jewish mentality, isn't that so?"

"Not at all. You don't think like a Jew. You think like a peasant. Your worries, your fears, your superstitions. That's how peasants think. Your mind is a thousand years old."

"You make me sound like the people who read *Tomorrow*. Do you actually believe that I think that way?"

"Not all the time, but sometimes."

"Then maybe my feelings about Lily are all wrong. I keep complaining about the way she treats me but everybody loves her. The super, the elevator man, the neighbors. I'm beginning to feel guilty."

He laughed again. "That's a sign of life with you. Guilt is your natural habitat."

I couldn't help laughing too.

"Don't despair," he said. "You still have your sense of humor."

"I have to tell you, doctor, that when I was a little boy, my favorite children's story was *Pinocchio*. And when I married Lily, I really believed that she was the Blue Fairy!"

"Many marriages start out the same way."

We both laughed.

"Which reminds me," I said, "that I haven't even mentioned what was uppermost in my mind when I came in. I have a feeling that Billy and Dawn are going to set a wedding date sooner than Lily expects. My son, David, doesn't agree with Lily that it's such a terrible thing and..."

"Next time, Mr. Flom. Our hour is up."

He still calls it an hour even though it lasts only forty-five minutes. It's like the pound of coffee that comes in a fourteen-ounce can. Still, it was good to know there would be a next time. I can't bear to think that Dr. Abel will soon be leaving for his vacation.

I appreciated him even more that evening. My mother was complaining about feeling "heavy" after eating so I took her to her doctor for a check-up. He's a geriatric specialist and his patients are almost exclusively Jewish. These patients have patience. They wait and wait. The always crowded waiting room could easily be mistaken for a *shul* on the eve of Yom Kippur.

But they love him because he calls them by their first name, pats them reassuringly no matter how sick they are, and tells them, "Let me do the worrying."

My mother doesn't let other people do her worrying. Unlike Lily's mother, she asks questions. With my mother, a doctor has to work for his money.

"No, it's not your angina," he told her. "Yes, it's your hiatal hernia. No, you don't have to take twice as many heart pills. Yes, you should eat lightly. No, you should stay away from salt. Yes, you can have all the cottage cheese you want. No, you don't need an operation. Yes, you'll feel better if you take this."

He handed her a prescription. On it was written the magic word *Maalox*, the Perrier Water of the over-65 population. It is so popular among Jewish people with heartburn that many think it's a Yiddish word for Good Health.

Afterward, I drove my mother over to my apartment for dinner. Lily met us at the door and asked, "How did you make out with the doctor?"

"All right. It's not her heart, knock wood," I said, rapping my knuckles against the bookcase in the hall.

She gave me a contemptuous look. "Does God know you're knocking on wood?"

"He knows."

"He knows it's real wood, not plastic that looks like wood?"

"He knows."

"How does he know?"

"He made it."

My mother laughed. "Joel's always been a little superstitious, Lily. He doesn't like to take chances."

"Did the doctor give you any medicine?"

"*Maalox*. I've taken it before but he forgets."

"Did it help?"

"Oh, sure."

"So why did you stop taking it?"

"I heard you can get kidney stones from taking too much."

"How much is too much?"

"Who knows?"

"So how much will you take?"

"I'll see."

After that exchange, she went into the kitchen and began emptying her shopping bag of delicacies she'd made for us: a jar of potato soup, a jar of beef flanken with sauerkraut, and a noodle pudding.

"That'll be our dinner," said Lily. "Now let's all sit down and eat."

"Wait," my mother said, taking a postcard out of her handbag. "Who do you think I heard from? Bertha."

Bertha was her niece, my cousin, and an absolute bitch. I have never heard a good word about Bertha from my mother. Still, she was obviously pleased to have heard from her, probably because Mom has so few living relatives. This kind of logic was something Lily could not understand.

"Well, I hope you aren't going to answer her," said Lily.

"I'll see."

"What do you mean, you'll see? She's no good. You know she's no good. You've told me a million times how mean she's been to you."

"She's always been like that."

"Just tear up the card and forget about it."

"You know what they say about people like her," my mother chuckled, "that they have the evil eye."

"You don't believe that, do you?"

"Do I believe it? Lily, you should know better."

"Good. Then tell her to go to hell."

"Why should I bother?"
"You're right. Just don't answer her."
"I'll send her a card for her anniversary."
"Why?"
"She sent me a nice postcard."
"Your move, Joel."
"Mom," I broke in, "that's just her way of getting over her guilt, for having been so mean to you."
"Believe me, she should have plenty of guilt."
"Then why do you want to send her an anniversary card?"
"Joel, I don't understand why you get so worked up over everything."
"I'm not worked up! But the way she treated you, I wouldn't talk to that bitch again."
"Who talks to her? She never even calls me."
"So why do you want to send her a card?"
"It will be her anniversary soon. Let her have a card."
"You should put poison in the envelope, all she ever did for you."
"She did for me?"
"Think about all you've done for her."
"You wouldn't believe it."
"Then don't send her a card!"
"Listen, it doesn't bother me."
"Soup's on!" yelled Lily, who'd been heating up our dinner while eavesdropping on our conversation and relishing every word. She loved to stir things up between

my mother and me. Then she pacified everybody with food.

Dinner was comparatively peaceful. We talked about our concern that Billy and Dawn might marry before they finished law school, but my mother's only comment was, "What should I wear to the wedding?"

After dinner, she said she wanted to go home to her own apartment because she had things to do. The first thing she did when we all arrived was to turn on her three little radios, one in each room.

"Mom, why do you have so many radios on?"

"Because I go from room to room," she said.

"So what?"

"They follow me."

"Who follows you?"

She pointed up. "Them."

"The neighbors upstairs?"

"They bother me, hammering on the wall, moving furniture, not letting me sleep, so I bother them."

"You mean they make noise at night?"

"No, during the day too. They follow me around from one room to another. If I go to the bathroom and flush the toilet, they flush the toilet."

"They aren't making any noise now," said Lily.

"That's because they know you're here. As soon as you go, they'll start. Then I'll turn up the radios real loud."

"You mean they only make noise when you're home alone?"

"That's right."

"Just to upset you?"

"They don't upset me."

"But the noise bothers you."

"Wouldn't it bother you if people made noise over your head all the time?"

My mother puzzled me. I had always known her to be a very rational person and I couldn't understand why her upstairs neighbors were deliberately annoying her.

"Did you have an argument with them, Mom?"

"Of course not. I never even talk to them."

"Maybe I should go upstairs and talk to them."

"Don't waste your time, Joel."

"But I can't have them bothering you like this. I have to do something."

"You don't have to do anything. Leave it to me."

"What are you going to do?"

"I'll show you."

She went into her kitchen and came out holding a broom. Then she looked up and started banging on the ceiling with the broom handle.

"Stop that!" I yelled. "They aren't doing anything up there."

"That's what you think," she said, banging away.

"Stop that, please! I'll go to the police. I'll tell them those people are harassing you. I'll do anything. Just quit banging on the ceiling like that."

She put down the broom reluctantly, saying, "As soon as you're gone, they'll start in again."

"Well, just as a favor to me, will you please try to ignore them?"

"You don't have to worry, Joel. I can take care of myself."

With that, my mother went to the kitchen to put back the broom.

I was reluctant to leave her home alone but Lily, who had stood by quietly, now said, "I think it's better that we leave her to her own devices. She's a very independent person and doesn't want us to interfere."

"You think she'll be all right?"

"She'll be fine. She always did have a powerful imagination and now it's running away with her."

"Lily! You're speaking of my mother! Be reasonable. Those upstairs neighbors could be noisy and you know that my mother is very sensitive."

"I know. But she's getting older. There is no reason why anyone would take the trouble to bother her the way she says."

"Maybe we don't know the reason. I think I'll plant a tape recorder in her apartment. Then we'll know what's what."

"I realize that you don't want to hear this, Joel, but I have a strong suspicion that your mother is becoming senile."

"Lily! How can you be so vicious? Why can't you express yourself more tenderly?"

"Knock it off. One day you'll be senile too."

That did it. I had run out of words. I was a beaten man with nothing more to say. I went into the kitchen, kissed my mother good night and we left.

When we got into the car and I started the motor, all I could say was, "What a day this has been."

And for some reason which I still cannot fathom, Lily began to sing, "It's a rare mood I'm in. Why, it's almost like being in love!"

She began to laugh. Then I began to laugh. A real laugh. A Dr. Abel laugh. It made absolutely no sense but I'm sad to say that it was fun, and I don't know why! Who cares!

*E*ven the newsroom at *Tomorrow* was becoming a fun retreat for me. Dr. Abel was right. The job did take me away from my problems — the place was cool, and the goings-on broke me up when I played back my tapes.

Suddenly, however, tumult was the name of the game. The place was in an uproar. Nancy, an ambitious new reporter, had written an "exclusive" story about a famous movie star dying of cancer and Levin had splashed it across the front page. Now the movie star, very much alive and without the disease, was threatening to sue. Levin was livid.

"What do you expect me to tell the publisher!" he raged.

On the verge of tears, she protested, "But, Levin, you knew that we had no real back-up to the story."

"You told me he went to the hospital complaining of stomach pains."

"That's right. And you said it must be cancer."

"What am I supposed to be, a doctor as well as an editor?"

"You told me to write it that way, like he had cancer."

"I told you to speculate, that's all."

"That's what I did. But the headline said he was dying of cancer. That's not in my story."

"Then you admit it's in the headline."

"But I didn't write the headline."

"Don't try to pass the buck, Nancy. I've been in this business a long time. It's my job to look out for the publisher's interests."

"Well, the issue sold like hotcakes. The publisher was happy."

"He's not going to be happy now."

"Why don't we just print a retraction in a little box?"

"We don't retract anything we print. That would destroy our credibility."

Desmond, calm and collected, approached Levin. "I have an idea. Why don't we have Nancy do a follow-up story?"

"An obituary, maybe?"

"Dear me, no. We simply up-date by running a new story plugging his latest movie with a great color shot of him headlined.

THE MAN WHO WOULDN'T DIE

He'll love it."

Levin's eyes sparkled. "We'll make him a hero, a real spunky guy who fought back against disease and death itself, and editorialize on how we admire his gutsiness. Great!"

I leaned over and whispered to Desmond, "That was positively brilliant."

"Thank you, Joel."

Levin's mood perked up considerably after that hassle. He was even receptive to Hubie, his favorite whipping boy, who was doing a column entitled 'Dear Phyllis' that dealt with readers' personal problems.

"I don't know how to answer this question you gave me, Levin. I need help."

"Read it to me, Hubie."

"This guy writes. 'Dear Phyllis. I have made my wife pregnant, my mother-in-law pregnant and my sister-in-law pregnant. What can I do now?'"

Levin gave a dirty laugh and said, "Tell him to go fuck himself!"

Everyone howled, and he basked in their appreciation.

"That's a great answer," said Hubie after recovering from a paroxysm of laughter, "but we can't print it."

"Okay. Dump the question and use another one. We don't have to deal with perverts."

His jovial attitude emboldened me to suggest a story that seemed promising.

"This might make page one. It's a breakdown by a top consumer expert on the most common frauds perpetrated on the public."

"Maybe you have something there, Flom. Our readers like that kind of stuff. Let me see your notes."

He read my notes, mumbling half-aloud, "Get your share of buried treasure... Send a dollar, get a diamond... Make a million in your spare time... Forget it, Flom. Kill it."

"You don't think it's a good story?"

"It's too good. You should read our paper more thoroughly. Every one of these is an advertiser."

I slunk off in shame and embarrassment. Worse, Levin was now his old nasty self again, screaming at everybody, especially me.

"We have to start thinking about a prophecy issue. We need some new predictions and some new psychics to make them. Anybody got any ideas? How about you, Flom?"

"I'm sorry, Levin. I don't know any psychics. Their predictions never come true anyway."

"If they make enough of them, some are bound to come true."

"What if they don't?"

"Nobody remembers. All that matters is that we give our readers something to believe in. Don't you see that yet, Flom? We sell dreams. Hope for the hopeless. That's our job."

I was about to ask another stupid question when Desmond saved me from making a complete fool of myself.

"What about that kid from Egypt, Levin? You know, the five-year old with the gift of seeing into the future. We used him once before and he went over big with our readers. He must be six by now."

"Can you get to him, Des?"

"I'm sure his mommy and daddy would be delighted. They had him on TV a few weeks ago and are living in Brooklyn. I have a feeling that they are quite hungry and interested in purchasing a co-op. I think if we offer them..."

"Give him a grand, okay?"

"Righto. That should do it."

"Good. We'll superimpose a shot of the kid in front of the pyramids. It'll make a great spread."

The words came out of my mouth before I could stop them. "You're going to have a six-year-old child foretell the future?"

"He's an Egyptian! Just make a list of things he can prophecy about. Breakthroughs in medicine, UFO landings, stuff like that, while Des works up some futuristic gossip about the stars. Not the stars in the sky, Flom, the movie and TV stars. Our readers will eat it up. A six-year-old prophet! We'll outsell everybody with this issue. It'll be like the Second Coming. I can't wait to tell the publisher. I'll call him right now."

He was absolutely transfixed when he went to the phone, a big grin across his face. I watched him, talking excitedly, animatedly, when suddenly his expression turned sour and he yelled, "Flom! The publisher wants to talk to you."

I grabbed the phone.

"Joel? Is that you? Are you there?"

"Yes, Harold."

"I had to talk to you. I've just finished reading your column and I think it's marvelous."

"Column? What column?"

"The one you call 'Notes From A UFO.' None of our competitors have anything like it. Not the *Enquirer*, not the *Star*, not the *Globe*. What a find you've made!"

I was overwhelmed. I'd written that column as a joke and had passed it around the newsroom for laughs. I used as a by-line the name Qrnk, with an editorial note that the author was a UFO visitor from outer space and that his name should be pronounced like a grunt because extra-terrestrials can't pronounce vowels. Somehow, the spoof must have reached Levin who took it seriously and passed it on to the publisher.

"Joel? Are you there? Can you hear me?"

"Yes, Harold. I've just been thinking about what you said, that's all."

"Say, you have come up with a really great idea. Our readers will love this column. Imagine, an actual correspondent from outer space. You will be able to contact this individual and do a column every week, won't you? Can I count on it? Is it possible?"

"Harold, I hate to say this, but there's nobody to contact."

"Well, whoever it is that you spoke to, what's his name, Qrnk. I'm not sure how to pronounce it."

"It's just a grunt, that's all. But..."

"Wonderful. I really like this stuff about how these UFO individuals keep an eye on us for our own good and mean us no harm. It really gives the reader a feeling of security to know that someone is looking after them."

I just didn't have the heart to tell him it was all a joke. He was on a high.

"The best thing I ever did, Joel, was asking you to join us," he went on enthusiastically. "Starting right now, I'm going to give you a big raise in salary to show my appreciation."

"That's very generous of you, Harold. I really don't know what to say."

"There's nothing to say. Just be sure to keep in touch with what's-his-name."

I grunted.

"Right! This is the biggest thing we've ever had going for us and I'm very grateful to you. I knew you had important contacts but never guessed that you had one like this."

I thanked him for his kind words and hung up in a daze. My head was spinning. Was my old college chum putting me on? Did he really believe there was a Qrnk?

How could he be so successful when I'd made honors in college and he hadn't even graduated?

But I didn't ruminate for long. No sooner had I put down the phone when Levin's voice boomed, "I want a headline for this story about the crowd that clapped their hands for eighty-four minutes at a rock concert. That's a record! Well, who's got a good headline for it?"

Still in shock from my conversation with the publisher, I blurted out, "How about

RECORD-BREAKING CLAP?"

Beside me, Desmond muttered, "Oh dear, oh dear."

Levin just stared at me balefully. "You have a dirty mind, Flom. Why don't you start using your head instead of your prick?"

I was shocked. The double-entendre aspect of my suggestion had never crossed my mind. Levin had the dirty mind, not I. Even Lily would agree with me, I was sure. Well, not exactly sure.

The subway was jammed. The air-conditioning wasn't working. And the train stopped so many times between stations I was afraid I'd have a panic attack. By the time I got home, I was perspiring and agitated. All I wanted was peace and quiet. Instead, when I got to the apartment I found the door was unlocked.

"Lily, you forgot to lock the door!"
"I thought I had."
"It's dangerous to leave it unlocked."
"Lock it now. Why are you home so late?"
"The train was slow."
"You probably stopped for a drink."
"I wish I had."
"Calm down and have your dinner. It's getting cold."

I did what she told me, calmed down and had my dinner. It was a great All-American meal. Steak, mashed potatoes, carrots and peas. I had to compliment her.

"What a wonderful meal that was, Lily. No tofu, no broccoli, no yogurt. Just good plain food."

"You have no class. I had to force myself to make a meal like that."

"I enjoyed every bite. And after you pour the coffee, I have some good news to tell you."

"You never have good news."

"The publisher is giving me a raise."

Her eyes lit up. It was wonderful to see.

"For that," she said, "instead of carrot cake, you get a brownie with your coffee."

She was about to give me one of her rare kisses when the doorbell rang. Company! And unannounced! I tensed up immediately.

"Don't be nervous, Joel. I'll go to the door."

In walked her cousin Flo with her husband, Sidney, a couple of real complainers, always full of *tsouris* and eager to pass it along to those they considered more fortunate, which was everybody.

"We were in the neighborhood and thought we'd stop by to say hello," said Sidney.

"How nice to see you," I lied.

Flo kissed me. Unlike Lily, she kisses everyone just because they're there.

"Sidney had to take me to the proctologist a few blocks from here," she explained to whomever was listening. "My colon's been acting up again."

"Sit down and have some cake and coffee," said Lily. "What did the doctor say?"

"He said it was spastic. He gave me all kinds of tests, but the worst was a proctoscope. You know where they do that."

"In the office," I said.

Lily gave me a dirty look.

"Did it hurt, Flo?"

"Let me tell you, Lily, if you never had a spastic colon, after a proctoscope you'll have one."

"But otherwise you're all right?"

"Thank God."

"How's your health, Sidney?" I asked out of politeness.

"I'm getting old, Joel. I can't pass a toilet without peeing."

"That's what toilets are for."

I couldn't help thinking that between her colon and his kidneys, we wouldn't see much of them this evening.

"How are the children?" asked Lily.

"Thank God," said Flo. "Alvin has given us a lovely granddaughter."

"And he has a wonderful father-in-law," added Sidney. "Very successful and very generous. When he buys himself a suit, he buys Alvin a suit."

"And Ronnie? What is he doing?"

"He's still trying to find himself."

"He lives at home with you?"

"Of course."

Life, Love and AudioTapes

"The trouble with Ronnie," said Sidney, "is that he can't make up his mind what he wants. I told him if you sit on a fence too long, you get splinters."

Straight out of the Talmud, I thought to myself.

"Does he still keep Kosher? He's still orthodox?"

"Certainly. That's how he was brought up. But now he drinks a beer and has some Gentile friends. What about your boys?"

"Well, David's working in the Catskills for the summer," said Lily, "and then he'll go back to medical school. Billy is working for a labor union in Boston and in September he'll go back to law school."

"How wonderful," said Flo enviously. "One son a doctor, another a lawyer. It's a mother's dream. Well, that's what comes of being married to a professional man, Lily. Are the boys going with anyone?"

"David is still looking, but Billy is living with a very nice girl."

"Living with her? They aren't sleeping together, are they?"

"I hope so."

"Well, as long as they're healthy," said Sidney quickly. "What's the girl's name?"

"Dawn."

"Dawn? A *shiksa*?"

"No, she's a nice Jewish girl. She and Billy go to law school together."

"She's going to be a lawyer too?" asked Flo, no longer able to conceal her envy. It made me very nervous.

"She isn't a lawyer yet," I said, hoping to counter the 'big eye' she was giving the kids. "She's still studying. Who knows what'll be?"

"Billy is so young," said Flo. "I can't believe he's really serious."

Lily just nodded. "We want him to wait until he graduates but they're in a big rush."

"So what's going to be?"

"We'll see."

"Does this girl come from a good family?" Sidney wanted to know. "What does her father do?"

"He's in the parking lot business."

That took the two of them by surprise. Finally, Flo said, "Well, it's honest work, parking cars."

Lily straightened them out at once. "What are you talking about? He owns parking lots, hundreds of them. He's a tycoon!"

By now they both were so devastated by envy I thought I'd die. Why couldn't Lily leave well enough alone and let them go on believing he parked cars!

"Would you like some more coffee?" she asked.

"No, thanks, we have to leave now," said Sidney. "I just want to go to the toilet."

He went, then she went. Then they both went. As soon as the door closed behind them, I began to mumble over and over again, "Oomp oomp oomp, oomp oomp oomp," to ward off the 'big eye.'

"I hear you, Joel. Now stop going through that ritual. It isn't going to help."

Who did she think she was, Dr. Abel?

At this crucial moment, the telephone began ringing. Lily picked it up, then turned to me. "It's Billy. Get on the extension. He wants you to hear this too."

Oh, my God! What now?

"Hi, Billy," I said, trying to be cool. "What's up?"

"Well, Dawn and I have talked things over and have decided to get married next month."

"You mean in August? This August?"

"Yes, before Labor Day."

Before Lily could get a word in, Dawn got on the line and said, "My mother is going to call you two. She and my father would like to meet you both when they come to New York. They're not sure exactly when but they'll let you know."

"Oh, you already told her of your plans?" asked Lily.

"I had to. She's making the wedding."

"Oh, of course. And she agrees that you should marry now, before you graduate?"

"She's all for it. So is my father. They don't understand why you object."

"We don't object, Dawn. You know that. We only thought... well, later."

Lily was flustered and Billy sensed it.

"Both of us are coming in this weekend. I called David and he's going to try to come in too, at least for a day, and we can all talk about it then."

"Goodbye for now," said Dawn.

Lily hung on to the phone, obviously overwhelmed.

"Hang up," I said.

She finally did, saying, "He didn't postpone the wedding like I told him to do."

"He's a big boy. He has to think for himself."

"Sure, I've done my job. I don't count any more."

"That's not true, Lily."

"It is true. Now he listens to Dawn's mother, not his own. I'm nothing."

"Oh no, you're everything. Take it from me. I know."

"You don't know anything. You're a man."

"Listen, Lily, if you're so upset, why don't you go and see Dr. Abel?"

"I wouldn't let him touch me!"

"He won't touch you. He's an analyst doctor, not a doctor doctor."

"Oh, you and your fancy words. Just remember, Billy is your son too. Why didn't you assert yourself!"

My first reaction was anger. My second reaction was guilt. My third reaction was shame. She was right. I had let her down. It was just too awful to contemplate.

There was no time to contemplate anything. Before I knew it, the weekend was upon us and the apartment overflowing with tension. I barely had time to tuck my tape recorder in an inconspicuous corner where it could quietly make family history.

Billy and Dawn had driven in early. David came in by bus and subway shortly afterward, but had to be back at the resort that evening. My mother was here. So was Lily's mother. That spelled trouble right away.

Whenever the two of them got together, each tried to out-do the other. I was a nervous wreck trying to keep tabs on who was winning. It was like watching a tennis match, my head turning first to this one, then to that one. Secretly, of course, I rooted for my mother. But if she came out ahead, I knew I'd have to deal with Lily and I couldn't bear to let her down again. Her mother got things off to a fast start.

"My teeth are killing me, Bea," she complained.

"Look at me, Frieda," my mother replied. "Three times I've been to my dentist and he still can't fix my bridge."

"At least you can chew."

"What can I chew? Hamburger?"

"I have to live on soft-boiled eggs."

"They're full of cholesterol."

"That doesn't get in my teeth."

"It gets in your blood, not your teeth."

"My blood doesn't hurt. My gums hurt."

"Then you need a gum man."

"I need a dentist."

"A gum man is a dentist. He's a specialist."

"I don't know what I'm going to do."

"Do what I tell you. Go to a gum man."

"I can't chew."

"Go see a gum man."

"I'm all washed out."

David was standing nearby, getting an earful. "Maybe it would be a good idea to consult a periodontist."

"See," said my mother triumphantly. "I told you."

"What's a perio?"

"That's a gum man."

Dawn, who had been spellbound by their conversation, suddenly sneezed.

"*Gezundheit*," said Lily's mother.

"Have you got a cold?" asked mine.

"No, I just sneezed."

"What are you taking for it?"

"Nothing. It's only a sneeze, maybe a touch of allergy, that's all."

"You'd better take something to drive it out," my mother advised. "What should she take, David? You're a doctor."

"Not yet, Grandma."

"All you need is a good cup of hot tea and you'll be all right," said Lily's mother, looking around her. "What happened to Billy? Where is he?"

"He's in his room rolling dope," said Lily.

"Oh, go on!"

"I'm only joking!"

"He shouldn't smoke that stuff," my mother said. "I heard it's very unhealthy. Am I right, David?"

"You're right, but Mom was kidding."

"I'd like to try some," said Lily's mother. "Maybe it would help my gums."

Lily tried to change the subject. "So what have you been doing at the Concord besides working, David?"

"I've been playing some golf. They have a beautiful golf course."

"That's nice."

"Didn't Bing Crosby drop dead on a golf course?" my mother asked.

Billy came into the living room just in time. He slapped me on the back and asked, "So what's this week's headline on *Tomorrow*, Dad?"

"It's an exclusive from the world's greatest seer, a six-year-old Egyptian with the gift of prophecy. **NEW HOPE FOR THE DEAD.**"

Everybody howled with laughter. Except Lily's mother.

"I can't wait to read it," she said, moving toward the bedroom. "It should be very interesting. Right now I think I'll take a little nap."

"I'll go look at the stove," said my mother, heading for her favorite haunt, the kitchen.

When the mothers were gone, Lily turned to Dawn and Billy and came right to the point. "About getting married before you graduate, I want to be sure you know what you're doing."

"We went over all that on the phone, Mom. Why do you keep bringing it up?"

"I'm just mentioning it. After all, getting married isn't like joining a health club. Don't you agree, Dawn?"

"Yes, but you don't have to be in love to join a health club. We're in love."

"If you're in love today, you'll be even more in love tomorrow. Look at Joel and me."

David shook his head. "Mom, they've made up their minds. It's their decision and you have to accept it."

"He's right, Lily," I said.

"You butt out!"

Billy held up his hands. "Please, stop all this. Let's calm down and do what we came here for, to discuss our wedding plans."

"Everything's all arranged?" asked Lily, a trace of bitterness in her voice but so subtle that only I, who know her longer than her children, could detect it.

"My mother's so excited she's already busy planning," said Dawn. "Billy and I prefer a casual family affair but she wants a big wedding with all the trimmings. She says a wedding is really for the bride's mother so we should let her have whatever she wants."

"Oh? How big a wedding is she planning?"

"Well, she started out figuring on at least 200 guests but she's trimmed it down to only 150."

"Only? You must have a lot of relatives and friends, and your father must have many business associates. We have a small family, a few close friends, and Joel doesn't have any business associates or friends. So there won't be too many coming from our side. Where will it be, Dawn, in your neighborhood *shul* or a catering hall?"

"Oh, mother's planning a house wedding."

"Your house can hold 150 people?"

"It's not going to be in the house. We have a great big garden beside the lake and we're going to set up a tent there."

"Like in the circus."

I winced.

"Won't it be awfully hot and humid in Florida in August?" I asked. "You can't have air-conditioning in a tent."

"It's not too bad by the lake," said Billy, "and you'll get a nice breeze coming from the ocean."

"I'll tell my mother to have fans put in the tent."

Lily was speechless.

Billy turned to David. "I want you to be my best man, okay?"

"You can count on it."

"Do you have a tux?" asked Dawn.

"A tux?"

"It's going to be a formal wedding."

"Oh no! You know how I hate to dress up."

"Me too," I groaned. "I never owned a tux in my life. Why does it have to be so formal?"

Lily rose to the occasion. "We'll rent tuxes, Joel. This is what Dawn's mother wants and it's her wedding."

"It's *my* wedding," said Dawn. "Gee, I didn't think this would be a problem. My father has a closet full of dinner jackets and everything."

"That's because your father is a businessman and goes to functions. Joel doesn't go anywhere except to the store."

My mother came out of the kitchen. "What's all the commotion here? Did someone get hurt?"

"Everyone is fine, Mom. We were just talking together."

"So loud, I thought someone got hurt."

Lily's mother shuffled in from the bedroom grumbling, "No use, I can't close my eyes. My teeth are killing me."

"Stop fooling around and go to a gum man," my mother admonished her.

The telephone began ringing.

"I'll bet that's my mother," said Dawn. "Should I get it?"

Lily nodded and Dawn walked over to the phone. It was her mother calling from Florida. "She wants to talk to you, Lily."

"Try to keep it down in there!" Lily called out nervously, taking the phone. Then, regaining her composure, she said sweetly, "Hello, Mrs. Burman... Mitzi? What a lovely name. And please call me Lily... Of course I'm delighted. At last we have a daughter..."

The conversation went on and on. I don't know what Mitzi said because I didn't have the tape recorder hooked into the phone but when Lily finally hung up, she said, "Your mother sounds like a very nice person, Dawn. She and your father are flying up next week to meet us."

Despite her seeming insouciance, I knew that Lily felt disenfranchised as a mother. I also knew that once she got her old zip back again, Mitzi would be no match for her. Without a doubt, there were anxious moments ahead.

Adding to my present anxiety was the awful realization that Dr. Abel would soon be leaving for his summer vacation. He would be away during August when I needed him most. To help prepare myself for this eventuality, I was spending my raise in salary for extra sessions because I needed all the treatment I could get.

"We had a full house this weekend, doctor. The whole family got together to discuss the wedding. It's going to be even earlier than we feared. This August. How do you like that?"

"It's as good a month as any for a wedding."

"But that's when you'll be away!"

"Rest assured that I'll be there in spirit, Mr. Flom."

"I hope so. The tension is already building up. Just watching the kids pack to go back to Boston drove me up a wall."

"Why did that make you tense?"

"Because they always forget things. A toothbrush, sunglasses, maybe a book. I have to keep after them so they don't forget."

"I see. You consider that your responsibility."

"Naturally. Lily says I'm a real Jewish father."

"She's only half right," he laughed. "You're a Jewish mother."

I had to think about that for a while, then I laughed too. But I reminded him, "It's Lily's fault. She should do the remembering if the kids don't, but she doesn't. So it's up to me. I always have to do things she should do. If I don't, I feel guilty because I know I should have. And no matter what I do, I'm never sure I did it right, that maybe I should have done it better or should have done it differently."

"Should should should. You suffer from what I call the tyranny of the 'should' — forever reviewing, doubting, second-guessing yourself. You're unable to make a decision without questioning it."

"You'd be the same way if you lived with Lily! She forces me to make the most ridiculous decisions and at the most ridiculous times, then pokes fun at me for making the wrong ones."

"You mean she plays games with you."

"Games, yes. Strange games. When we go to bed, she'll put out the light and play a game she calls Choices. She asks me questions. 'What would you rather have, a stroke or a heart attack? Lung cancer or a brain tumor?

A wooden arm or a wooden leg?' That's some game, huh?"

"It would make a good television quiz show."

"I'm serious, doctor. Games like that get on my nerves."

"Do they ever lead to anything interesting?"

Suddenly, I felt embarrassed. "You mean...?"

"Yes."

"Well, yes."

"In psycho-sexual jargon, that is known as foreplay. How's the main event? Pleasurable?"

"Well, yes. To be perfectly frank, you know those *yentas* you said I had in my head? They disappear after sex."

"That's a good sign. Playing Choices with your wife and losing is better for your mental health than playing any other game and winning."

I felt good about that, but time was fleeting and I had to get some help about my main problem before this session was over.

"Let's get back to the wedding, doctor. I have a big decision to make and I should have brought this up earlier."

"There goes that 'should' again. What decision do you have to make?"

"Well, it's going to be a gala affair at the in-laws' estate in Florida. I said estate!"

"I heard you."

"Their house is a palace right beside a lake. The grounds are so big that they're going to set up a tent, with electric fans to keep it cool, for the ceremony and reception."

"It sounds like an occasion not to be missed."

"There'll be 150 guests."

"Good. You'll have a lot of company."

"Not from my side."

"That's even better."

"The in-laws are flying in this coming week to meet us."

"It makes good sense to meet them before the wedding."

"You don't understand. We're the hosts. Where are we going to take them?"

"Invite them to your home for dinner."

"To a four-and-a-half room apartment in Queens? It's not like their home. Besides, one of our nosey neighbors could come in at any time, or the toilet could get stuffed and we'd have to call the super. What kind of impression would that make?"

"Why do you have to make an impression? Your son is a good catch. He'll be a big lawyer one day."

"The biggest. But that's not in the here and now. Lily says we should take them out to dinner at a good restaurant."

"So your problem is solved."

"Solved? Do you know how many restaurants there are in New York?"

"You only need one."

"But it has to be the right one."

"I don't think they're going to be as concerned as you and your wife are. They just want to get acquainted."

"You make it sound so simple."

"It is simple. Since these people are not New Yorkers, they might enjoy visiting a restaurant that's popular with New Yorkers."

"You mean an 'in' place."

"Right."

"They'll love that. Why didn't I think of that myself? I shouldn't have needed your help. I should have thought of it when Lily first got on the phone with Dawn's mother. We should have set the time and place right then."

"Again, Mr. Flom, you've bowed to the tyranny of the 'should.'"

"Oh, I didn't realize it."

"We just went over it."

"Then I should have known better."

"There you go again."

"How am I going to get over this habit?"

"We'll have to work on it... go over it again."

And again and again and again. Lily would be no help. I know what she'll say when I tell her what Dr. Abel suggested. She'll say, "Can't you make any decisions without his help? You *should!*"

I wasn't too far off the mark. When I told her that Dr. Abel had suggested that we take the Burmans to an 'in' restaurant, she looked at me contemptuously and said, "You should be ashamed of yourself! You even need an analyst to tell you where to eat."

"Well, *you* couldn't decide where to go either."

"But I know where to turn for help, and it's not an expensive analyst."

She waved a newspaper clipping in my face. "See, I don't need to have my head examined to pick a restaurant. All I need is guidance from an expert. And this one lists his favorite spots for entertaining out-of-towners. There are only three we've eaten at — the *Palm*, *Lutece* and the *Coach House*."

"We can skip the *Palm*. The steaks are great but it's too crowded and noisy for this occasion. And we can skip *Lutece* because we can only afford to eat there when somebody else picks up the check. The *Coach House*

Lily & Joel

sounds good and it's in Greenwich Village, not far from Dr. Abel's office."

"I knew that would appeal to you. If you get an anxiety attack in the middle of dinner, you can hop right over to your guru."

She was right, of course. The thought had indeed crossed my mind. Meeting my son's future in-laws for the first time posed a situation so fraught with anxiety that just knowing that Dr. Abel was nearby made me feel more secure.

We were pretty sure that the Burmans had never been to the *Coach House* and probably wouldn't dream of setting foot in Greenwich Village, a locale that out-of-towners think is restricted to hippies, hopheads and homosexuals. In fact, Dawn had told us that whenever her parents visited New York, they always stayed in midtown within the bounds of *Saks Fifth Avenue* and *Bloomingdale's*. So when Lily phoned Mitzi to tell her where to meet us, I warned her not to say it was in Greenwich Village, but on Waverly Place off Fifth Avenue, which has a more impressive ring to it, and that we'd have a table waiting.

Lily and I arrived early to be sure we had a good table. We did. It was on the balcony overlooking the downstairs dining room, away from the crowd. I was able to hide my tape recorder between my feet in the darkness under the table without Lily noticing me sneaking it down there.

"Did you take your *Valium*, Joel?"

"No. Let's have a drink."

"Not before they get here."

"I need it now."

Before she could stop me, I ordered a martini on the rocks. The minute the waiter brought it, I took a big swallow.

"That's right, Joel. Get drunk. That'll make a good impression. Well, what do you care about your son."

"If I didn't care, I wouldn't be here."

"If we had a penthouse on Park Avenue, we wouldn't have to be here."

"Ssshhh! Look down, over the railing. That must be them coming in now."

"What makes you think so?"

"Look at those tans. That's not from a sunlamp. They look like a pair of bronze bookends. See, they're talking to the maitre'd and he's pointing up here."

"I'll wave to them."

"She's waving back. Hey, Dawn's mother isn't bad to look at."

"Watch your drinking, Joel!"

"Don't worry. You don't have to be jealous."

"Jealous? Her father looks much younger than you and he's dressed better too."

"Well, you picked out what I'm wearing."

"It's your only suit that's still in style. Pull up your tie."

"I can't. I'll choke."

"Well, do it quietly. Here they come."

The martini was beginning to work. I was in a good mood and ready for them.

"Hi. I'm Joel and this is Lily."

"Glad to meet you. I'm Chuck and this is Mitzi."

They sat down and I immediately ordered a round of drinks for everybody, including me.

"What a lovely room," said Mitzi.

"This place was a carriage house in the old days," said Lily, "and we're sitting up here in what used to be the hayloft. And down there... oh, my God, look!"

"What's the matter!" I exclaimed. "What are you pointing at? Is something flying around?"

"Craig Claiborne just came in!"

"Who is he?" asked Mitzi. "A friend of yours?"

"I wish he was. He's one of the world's greatest food connoisseurs. What a thrill it is to see him here."

Lily was so happy. I felt so glad for her. While she blabbered on enthusiastically to Mitzi, I turned to Chuck and asked, "How's the parking lot business these days?"

"Very good."

"Dawn told us you have parking lots all over the country. Do you have any in New York?"

"Not yet. There's no space available. We'd have to buy out other lots. But we're working on it. Do you have many parking lots in your neighborhood, Joel?"

"Just a small one, but it's pretty far from our apartment."

"I suppose you keep your car in an indoor garage."

"No, we keep it on the street."

"Oh? Well, that's probably more convenient."

"Not if it's parked in one of the alternate-side-of-the-street spots because the next morning you'll be on the wrong side and you can't leave it there between eight and eleven. When that happens, Lily has to go down early and move the car so we won't get a ticket. Still, it's cheaper than..."

"I can't tell you how thrilled we are to have Dawn as a daughter-in-law," Lily almost shouted, cutting me off. "She's a wonderful girl."

"Well, you have a terrific son in Billy," said Mitzi, "and I hear your other son is going to be a doctor. That's a rare combination. Two brothers, both professionals."

"Yes. Thank God they're not creative."

Mitzi gave her a puzzled look but said nothing.

"Let's order," I said, picking up the menu. "What do you think, Lily, should I have the smoked turkey with the nitrites or the lobster with the cholesterol?"

"On special occasions like this, Joel, health doesn't count. Eat what you like now and worry later."

After we all ordered, Lily got down to business.

"Are you planning an orthodox wedding, Mitzi?"

"Oh no, we're Americanized."

"That's nice. Then the men won't have to wear *yarmulkes?*"

"Skullcaps we call them in Florida. Chuck's friend, Bill Blass, is designing them in contemporary Jewish. If anyone wants to wear them, fine. But they're really for the guests to take home as souvenirs."

"Designer *yarmulkes*. How charming. Will you have a rabbi presiding?"

"Three rabbis."

"Three?"

"Yes. The rabbi from our regular reformed temple, the old rabbi who bar-mitzvahed Chuck, and the company rabbi."

"You have a company rabbi?" I asked Chuck.

"Indeed we do, Joel. It's good for business. Every evening he blesses all the parking lots. I know it sounds ridiculous but our Jewish clientele loves it and so do our Gentile customers. They feel their cars will be protected."

I gulped down the last of my martini and tried to imagine a rabbi making a *brocha* over a lot full of automobiles. A rabbi like that would be featured in *Tomorrow* if we put out a Jewish edition.

"Are you going to serve Kosher food?" Lily asked.

"No, I'm planning a gourmet dinner, French style. I hope that won't be a problem for your family."

"Not at all. We're Americanized too."

I couldn't help thinking of how Lily's mother served everything from tea to highballs in *Yahrzeit* glasses or jelly jars, but decided not to bring it up.

"I'm having a French caterer," Mitzi went on, "so the meal will be very special. Naturally, we'll start with French champagne, and then there'll be a different

French wine matched to every course. We'll finish with a flourish, a magnificent French dessert table. How does that sound to you, Lily?"

"Sounds super. French wine, French desserts, French bread, French everything."

"Except bread."

"No French bread?"

"No bread at all, and no butter. That eliminates the need to serve bread plates so there'll be more room on the tables."

"You could put the bread on the dinner plates."

"No, my caterer said bread is unfashionable with a real French dinner."

"Really? I never knew that. Where is your caterer from? Paris?"

"Oh no. Palm Beach. He has a fantastic background. When he first started out, he had the best bagel bakery in Miami. But then he went continental and switched to croissants. That made his reputation and now he's in Palm Beach."

Lily smiled agreeably. The evening proceeded nicely. The Burmans said the pecan pie we ordered for dessert reminded them of home. After I paid the bill and tipped the waiter, we all exchanged kisses and handshakes and the Burmans took a cab to their hotel. Lily and I took the subway.

"You certainly ate a lot," I said to her.

"I ate for my nerves. Why didn't you stop me?"

"You were enjoying yourself. That made me happy."

"Well, I'm not happy. I'll have to get a good virus now to lose weight."

"Don't say things like that."

"I think she's making a big mistake."

"Who? What are you talking about?"

"Mitzi said she's not serving bread."

"So what?"

"They always serve French bread at a French dinner."

"What makes you so sure now? When she brought it up, you said you didn't know."

"What I said then doesn't count. What I say now counts. And I say they do serve bread."

She said it very forcefully. This wasn't going to be her last word on the subject, not if I know Lily. And I do. Sometimes.

The bustling newsroom of *Tomorrow* distracted me from ruminating about Lily and the wedding. My friend the publisher was right about 'Notes From A UFO.' Readers loved the column. Supermarkets were selling out their copies of the paper as fast as they stacked it on their racks. The mail on my desk was piling up, most of it addressed to Qrnk.

While I was poring over the letters, Levin came over and said, "Got a lot of good stuff there, Flom?"

"Very positive, Levin."

"I've got an idea."

"That's great."

"How do you know? You didn't hear it yet."

"I mean, it's great that you have an idea," I said lamely, realizing that I'd given him a knee-jerk response like a real toady.

"Ideas are my business," he growled. "They're the lifeblood of this paper. That's why I'm in charge. What

I want you to do is pick out the best letters for a center spread."

"Two full pages of letters?"

"Now you've got it. Reader participation, see? We encourage them to correspond with Qrnk in outer space. Well?"

"Oh, I'm sure we'll have more than enough letters."

"Good. We'll dress it up with some great pictures."

"Pictures?"

"Yeah, of a UFO and maybe Qrnk himself."

"But there is no Qrnk. I made him up."

"Our readers don't know that or they wouldn't be writing to him, would they?"

His logic was overwhelming.

"We have plenty of shots of flying saucers in the files, Levin, but…"

"We need a being! Can't we get a being, Flom? Think!"

I had to think fast.

"Well, I heard from a reader who claimed she was entertaining a visitor from outer space. And just to keep her happy I asked if she could send us a photo. But she told me that extra-terrestrials don't register on film. The only thing that would show is an aura."

"An aura. Kind of a halo, I guess, what the psychics call an emanation. Hey, that might do it. Get in touch with this gal and have her take a picture of her front door showing the aura where the extra-terrestrial is standing. Offer her a hundred bucks for the picture."

"Suppose the aura doesn't show up?"

"Then we'll air-brush it in. That makes sense, doesn't it?"

He was so convincing that I found myself nodding in agreement. But then I saw the flaw in the plan.

"Wait a minute, Levin. The aura isn't Qrnk."

"That's right. It's a friend of Qrnk, sent here by him as a gesture of good will."

"It sounds so unbelievable."

"Everything is unbelievable until you set it in type. When will you learn?"

He had a way of making me feel stupid.

"Do we have a Mr. Gravis working here?" came an unexpected yell from the switchboard operator.

"It's the wrong number," Levin yelled back.

"He says he's calling about the Disease-of-the-Week series we've been running and Mr. Gravis wrote one."

Suddenly it came to me.

"He means myasthenia gravis. That's a disease, not a person."

"Goddamn idiot." muttered Levin. "Talk to him, Flom."

I picked up the phone.

"Mr Gravis?" the caller asked.

"No, there is no Mr. Gravis," I said patiently.

"Excuse me, I have your paper right here. He must be a Greek, first name spelled M-y-a-s-t-h-e-n-i-a. That's wrong?"

"No, sir, that's right. But he's not a Greek. He's a disease. I mean, myasthenia gravis is a disease."

"I have a question."

"I'm sorry, but we don't take questions on the telephone. You'll have to send us a letter with your question."

"Okay. Should I send it to Mr. Gravis?"

"No, no. Just send it to Disease-of-the-Week in care of *Tomorrow*."

"You'll see that he gets it?"

"I'll see to it personally."

By this time, my brain was reeling. I had to reorient myself to reality. It wasn't easy. It never is. I suppose that's why it's called reality.

My sense of reality returned with a jolt at my next therapy session. Something was wrong with Dr. Abel. I knew it the minute I saw his face. His usual tranquil expression was missing. His nose was red. His eyes were tearing. He sneezed and coughed. Never before had it occurred to me that an analyst could get sick. It was a fearsome discovery.

"You don't look well, doctor," I said anxiously.

"It's just a little cold."

"This is a terrible time to be sick."

"Summer colds clear up faster than winter colds."

"I hope so. You know, this is a crucial time for me. You'll soon be leaving for your vacation."

"I'll be back before you know it."

"With God's help."

"I appreciate your prayers."

"My prayers?"

"You're rocking back and forth like you're *davvening*."

"It's just my way of expressing my deepest feelings."
He blew his nose.

"Are you listening to me, doctor?"

"Every word."

"You don't seem as attentive as usual."

"I had to blow my nose. Excuse me. Now please go on, Mr. Flom. I can see there's something bothering you."

"Well, my mother is behaving peculiarly."

"Oh?"

"She has cockroaches in her kitchen."

"In New York that's not uncommon."

"Wait. I brought her a can of roach spray. Then two days later I dropped in to see her and found the can empty."

"Good. The roaches were gone."

"Not really. So I brought her another can and dropped in the next day to see how she made out. And would you believe it, she'd emptied the entire can in one day."

"I suppose some roaches are more resistant than others."

"That's not the point. The point is that she had both empty cans lined up under the sink. When I offered to throw them out, she said, 'No, I'll take care of it.' What could I do?"

"Buy her a third can."

"That's what I did."

"You're a good son."

"I'm an only child. She has no one else."

"As long as she has you, she doesn't need anyone else."

"But she won't throw away any of the empty cans. Don't you think it's peculiar to hoard empty roach spray cans?"

"Not for your mother."

"How many cans of spray does a person need to get rid of a few lousy roaches?"

"I don't know," he laughed. "I'm a psychiatrist, not an exterminator."

"All right, I agree the story sounds ridiculous, but I'm truly worried about my mother. Whenever I question her about hoarding the empty cans, she gets annoyed with me."

"She's not annoyed, she's perplexed. I'm afraid she's getting old, Mr. Flom."

"You don't have to be so blunt, doctor. But I guess it's true, she does get mixed up. Right after she heard that Billy was getting married, she asked me if he's going out with anybody yet."

"I'm surprised you haven't mentioned your meeting with the future bride's parents. How did it go?"

"So far, so good. They're normal people like us."

"I'm glad to hear it."

"Where we differ is that they're real straight, while Lily and I are romantics. You know, like Jeanette Macdonald and Nelson Eddy."

"You see Lily as Jeanette Macdonald and you as Nelson Eddy?"

"Yes, except that we have a more meaningful relationship than they ever had, even when he sang to her. They never looked at each other."

"Not like you and your wife."

"Not at all. I always look at Lily and she always looks at me. In fact, sometimes she over-does it and I feel like I'm being scrutinized."

"As though you were on trial."

"That's it! And I'll tell you something else, doctor. Lots of times, she stares at me and makes fun of the way I'm dressed or the way I comb my hair. And what makes me really angry is that when I ask her why, she belittles me. She says, 'Because I like to torment you.' Just like that. She actually admits it!"

"You're a lucky man. Your wife doesn't keep you guessing."

I began to squirm uneasily.

"Look, doctor, I'm ashamed to say this, but I have to get it off my chest. There have been times when Lily has gotten me so mad that I forgot myself and told her to drop dead. Oh, my God! Can you imagine my saying a thing like that? God forbid anything should happen to her!"

"Relax, Mr. Flom. When a Jew says 'drop dead,' he doesn't mean permanently."

What a revelation. I was so relieved that I didn't hear him say our time was up or remember to turn off the tape recorder. I was enjoying such a grateful release from guilt that only when Dr. Abel blew his nose did I snap out of my blissful state. I knew it couldn't last.

When I arrived home, I rang the bell as usual to make Lily come to the door and play our little game of 'Don't you have a key?' and 'I didn't want to scare you.' I rang and rang, but this time she didn't answer. She *had* to be home. It was dinner time. Oh my God, maybe she did drop dead after all!

My fingers trembled as I fumbled with the damn key, trying to unlock the door, and I finally burst into the apartment screaming, "Lily! Lily! I didn't mean it!"

"Ssshhh!" she said, glaring at me. "Can't you see I'm on the telephone?"

I was so relieved to see her alive and well that I went over to her and planted a big kiss on her forehead. She poked me in the ribs with her elbow and hissed, "Get away," then quickly changed her tone and said into the phone, "No, not you, Uncle Louie. I was talking to Joel... Oh, yes, that was a wonderful meal you and Aunt Bella prepared for us when we visited you. How did you like the *kugel* I made for you?... Uh-huh. No, I know it's not

French but I thought you'd enjoy one of my specialties... Yes, it's an old family recipe... Eastern European, right... Well, we'll look forward to seeing you both again real soon. Goodbye."

When she got off the phone, I said, "I told you that *kugel* wasn't his idea of haute cuisine."

"I'll guarantee that they ate up the last crumb."

"Well, maybe. But I still think we should have brought wine."

"Anybody can bring wine, Joel, but not everyone can make *kugel*. Now what were you screaming about when you came in?"

"I was worried about you because you didn't come to the door. I thought something had happened to you."

"You'd like that, wouldn't you?"

"Lily! That's a terrible thing to say. I swear, sometimes I don't understand you."

"If you understood me, you wouldn't want to live with me. Here, some letters came today from David and Billy. Nothing important. I'll prepare dinner while you read them and then you can throw them away."

"Are you crazy? You know I save them."

"What for?"

"They're from our kids, that's what for. I've got all their letters, from camp, from college, all of them."

"No wonder you need an analyst. I wish you were more like Chuck Burman."

"Rich, you mean."

"That's part of it. All you ever think about is the kids, never about me. Mitzi called me today. That made me think about me, the life I lead."

"What did she call you about?"

"She's having the wedding invitations printed and wants to know how many we'll need."

"We didn't even put together a guest list yet."

"That won't take long."

"Let's do it now. Dinner can wait. Get a pencil and paper."

"You'd better think this through carefully, Joel."

"I am. Let's start with the family. Just remember, at a wedding like this we can only invite acceptable relatives."

"That doesn't leave much to choose from, certainly not from your side."

"If I asked any of my relatives, I'd charge them admission. Whenever they invited my family to dinner, my father brought the food."

"Now we come to my side."

"Your side is no better, except for your Uncle Louie and Aunt Bella. At least they have some class. That takes care of the relatives. Now what about friends?"

"What friends?"

"How about some of your associates in the School Volunteers?"

"They're away for the summer — on the Riviera, in the Cotswolds, at Martha's Vineyard. They don't live like you and me, Joel."

Life, Love and AudioTapes

"I'm in no mood to argue, Lily. Let's finish."

"So far we have six people, including you and me, the groom, the best man, and my aunt and uncle."

"You forgot our mothers."

"I don't want to take them to the wedding."

"What are you talking about? They're our mothers."

"They went to our wedding, that's enough."

"We can't leave them out, Lily."

"Why not? We'll tell them it's a small wedding."

"But it's not a small wedding. It's an extravaganza. This is the biggest thing in their lives, seeing one of their grandsons married in such splendor. How can you be so heartless?"

"You'd be surprised."

"Billy will be unhappy, and so will David."

"They'll be relieved."

"I can't believe what I'm hearing."

"Joel, I'll be a nervous wreck all day and night worrying about what my mother is going to say next to embarrass me. And in that loud voice of hers."

"I agree with you. But we can't leave her home and just invite my mother."

"That's right. So let's leave them both home."

"Leave my mother home? She won't say anything to embarrass you."

"No, but she won't be able to eat this or eat that. You'll have to look after her all the time. But I suppose that's what you like. That's your idea of happiness."

"Wait a minute, we're not finished. Where are you going? I don't want dinner yet."

"I'm not going to make dinner. We'll talk about this later. Right now I think there's still time to call the French Embassy."

"What for?"

"Uncle Louie said they *do* serve bread with a French dinner. I have to know for sure."

"But the French Embassy? This isn't a state dinner."

"They'll know. Just mind your own business. If you haven't anything else to do, take out the garbage while I make my call."

Once again, she had the upper hand. She had the French Embassy and I had the garbage. I'm sure that even Dr. Abel would agree that it was an uneven exchange.

There isn't time or space enough here for all the transcribed tapes of our arguments about the guest list. Lily was adamant about not inviting our mothers and I was adamant about her shameless lack of feeling. The conflict seemed insoluble unless we got help from a third party. We did.

It was no secret to either of us that Lily's mother had little patience for cooking, so whenever we paid her a visit Lily brought along some cooked food. This time it was soup and chicken, some leftover beef stew, mashed potatoes and the ever-present *kugel*.

When Lily went to the range to heat up the soup and chicken, the gas didn't come on. I figured the pilot light was out so I put a match to it, but it didn't take. I sniffed around. No sign of gas.

"Hey, Ma," said Lily. "The stove doesn't work."

"Joel will fix it."

"He can't fix it. There's no gas coming through. When did you use the stove last?"

"I make coffee."
"But you use an electric percolator, don't you?"
"All the time. It's very nice. You just plug it in."
"What about food? Don't you cook at all?"
"If I have the time. I'm shot."

I spotted an unopened envelope from the gas company on the kitchen cabinet. "What's this letter?"

"Who knows? Advertisements. I don't bother with them."

Lily took the envelope and opened it.

"Ma, they turned off your gas a month ago because you didn't pay your bill!"

"Leave it to them."

"Didn't you know your gas had been turned off?"

"How would I know?"

"Well, how have you been eating?"

"I don't *potchky* around here. I go down the street for a bite. Maybe a little ice cream for my gums."

"What do you eat at home?"

"I open a can of tuna when it's on sale."

Lily was distraught. She took me aside, whispering, "She's getting worse, Joel."

"She's getting senile, like you said about my mother."

"Your mother cooks. Mine doesn't do anything. What should I do?"

"Turn on the gas."

"Joel!"

"I mean, pay the gas bill."

"What good is that if she won't turn it on?"

"Then take her back to the doctor."

"I took her last week."

"You never told me. What happened?"

"Nothing happened. While she was lying on the examining table waiting for the doctor, she kept staring at the supplies on his shelves, urging me out loud, 'There must be something here you need. Paper towels, cotton swabs, iodine. Take something. He'll never miss it.' Thank God she didn't say it in front of the doctor."

"Imagine what she's going to say at the wedding."

"I'm not through with that subject."

"Well, what did the doctor say was wrong with her?"

"All he said was she doesn't eat enough."

"She'll eat plenty at the wedding."

"I don't want to hear another word about the wedding!"

Suddenly, her mother, who'd been nibbling on the *kugel*, came to life. "I heard you mention the wedding. When is it?"

"Not until next month."

"Good. June weddings are lucky."

"June was last month. Next month is August."

"It'll be hot. I'll have to dress light."

"Ma, I'm sorry, but you won't be coming to the wedding."

"Why not? I'm not invited?"

"Of course you're invited. But Pop died only a short while ago and I know you wouldn't want to go without him."

"Who said so? It'll do me good."

"But how would it look for you to go so soon after Pop died?"

"He'd want me to go. Stop worrying, I'll be there."

That settled it. Lily took the pot of soup and chicken to the next-door neighbor's apartment and heated it up. She told her mother we'd have the gas turned back on and that she should remember to use the stove. Then we went home without saying another word about the wedding.

No sooner did we get into our apartment when the telephone rang. Lily took the call and handed me the phone. "It's your mother. Enjoy yourself."

"Hi, Mom," I said. "Everything all right?"

"What should be wrong? I just called to tell you I tried out the bed board you put under my mattress."

"Good. How does the mattress feel now?"

"I don't know."

"Well, it should feel firmer."

"Who told you that?"

"You did. You said a bed board would make the bed feel firmer."

"That's because the coils in the spring are sagging."

"Yes, that's why the mattress felt soft."

"Well, I have a firm mattress."

"But if the springs are sagging, it would feel soft. Doesn't the board make it feel firmer?"

"You're getting all worked up again, Joel."

"I'm not worked up!"

"Call me back when you calm down. I just wanted to let you know I tried out the bed board. My goodness."

By the time she hung up, I was in one of my nervous sweats. I put down the phone, it rang again.

"Oh, no!"

"Give it to me," said Lily.

It was Mitzi calling. I poured myself a scotch and soda. Lily pointed to the glass and then to herself. My Lily? I made her one. Let them talk. I had to cut out. Enough aggravation for one day! I went into the kids' room and shut the door, sipping my drink and lighting up.

Peace. For a short while. When I finally came out for a refill, Lily was just hanging up.

"That was Mitzi," she said, "bringing me up to date on the wedding."

"I figured as much. Did you tell her our mothers are coming?"

"All right, so you won! Do you want to hear what Mitzi had to say or don't you?"

"I do, I do. Hey, that's what I said when we got married!"

"Don't remind me. Mitzi wanted me to know what she's going to wear for the wedding. An original, of course."

"What does that mean?"

"That means it's going to be designed exclusively for her and will be very expensive. She's going to send me a swatch of the material so that I can wear something different. What a joke."

"Why is it a joke?"

"Because Mitzi will have something made to order by Bill Blass while I pick something off the rack at Loehmann's."

"You'll look spectacular in anything you wear."

"Sure, that's how you get off. With compliments. Every time I talk to her, I feel like a hardship case."

"You're not being fair to yourself."

"I don't live in a dream world like you. I believe everyone is lying when they say something good about me."

"Is that my Lily talking like that?"

"That's your Lily."

"You mustn't think that way. Mitzi lives a different kind of life, that's all."

"I know. My mother wanted me to have a life like that."

"I'll keep trying."

"She really didn't want it for me. She wanted it for herself."

"Take my word, no matter what you wear, you'll be the belle of the ball, a sensation."

"You may be right, considering what I'm thinking of wearing."

"What's that?"
"A nurse's uniform. Our mothers are coming."
"Very funny."
"Don't take another drink, Joel!"
"I'll do whatever I want."
"I said no."
"Well, I said yes."
"That's the second time you went against me, Joel. I don't like what's happening to you. I'm losing my control over you. That analyst is curing you and I don't like it!"

Oh, if only it was true.

*I*f it wasn't true, I was headed for big trouble. The day had come that I dreaded most, my last session with Dr. Abel before he left for his vacation. No more treatment until after Labor Day. I would be at the mercy of the THI, Lily, and the anxiety of coping with the wedding.

In this session, every second counted. I raced into the office, snapped on my tape recorder and immediately began blabbering.

"Calm down, Mr. Flom. I'm not running away."

"Oh, but you are. As soon as our time is up."

"I'll only be gone for a month."

"To me it'll be a lifetime."

"Before you know it, I'll be back. And who knows, you may not even need me any more."

"You sound like Lily. She said you're curing me."

"I'm glad to hear it."

"She also said she doesn't like the idea because it means that she's losing control over me."

"Do you agree with her conclusion?"

"Well, I won a small victory."

"For you, no victory is small. What did you win?"

"I convinced her that our mothers should be invited to the wedding. She was so against it that I never thought she'd give in. You know, Lily has a mind of her own. She doesn't like to be contradicted."

"I'm sure there are exceptions to that rule."

"Not many, doctor. She'll go out of her way to prove her point. When Billy's future mother-in-law said it wasn't proper to serve bread at a French dinner, Lily disagreed and actually called the French Embassy to prove she was right. And she was."

"You married a very resourceful woman."

"Listen, the whole thing was none of her business. She wasn't making the wedding. The trouble with her is that she can't keep her nose out of other people's business."

"I see."

"No, you don't see. You have to live with her to understand what I'm saying."

"We can't all be that lucky."

"Don't laugh."

"I'm not laughing."

"I don't know how I'm going to get along without you, doctor. This wedding is going to be a very anxious occasion for me. What will I do without you to reassure me?"

"Make a *brocha*."

151

"A *brocha*?"

"A little prayer. You've often told me how your grandmother used to have you make a *brocha* in times of crisis when you were a child, and it made you feel less anxious."

"You're right. My beloved grandma used to make me get up on a footstool and reach up to the chandelier in the living room and pray whenever she heard a clap of thunder, or when my mother and father had an argument, or when anybody was sick. How well I remember."

"And you're still making *brochas*."

"But that's not the way to solve problems."

"One day you'll really believe it."

"I hope so. But remember, doctor, my wife isn't as understanding as you are. She can say things that send me into a rage. Like the other day when I complained that Levin embarrassed me at the office, she criticized me for not speaking up. She told me I should have told him off."

"Let's you and him fight."

"That's it. And whenever she talks to me like that, we have an argument. So what's the answer?"

"Stop arguing."

"Don't blame me. I don't argue."

"You're arguing now."

"Who's arguing? I'm merely disagreeing with you."

Dr. Abel shook his head, then began to write on one of his prescription pads. He tore off the page and handed it to me. "Here, memorize these two words."

I read the note aloud: "You're right."

"Those are the magic words to keep in mind, Mr. Flom."

"But what if she's wrong?"

"Say them anyway."

"I wouldn't be true to myself."

"She'll never suspect it."

I stuffed the note in my pocket and asked anxiously, "Do you really think it'll work?"

"Give it a chance. It can't hurt. Good luck at the wedding. I'll see you after Labor Day."

"With God's help."

He laughed and looked up at the ceiling. I started to laugh, too, but when I looked up all I could think of was my mother and her neighbors upstairs.

With great reluctance, I wished him a happy vacation and made him give me his telephone number at Martha's Vineyard... in case of an emergency.

I was on my own.

𝓑e it ever so humble there's no place like home if there's no one around to bother you. I felt good because it was Saturday and Lily was out and it was very peaceful. I felt guilty because she was out shopping with our mothers to help them pick clothes for the wedding.

R-r-r-rrring!

Oh, that damned telephone. I had to pick it up.

"Hello."

"Oh, is that you, Joel?" came a cheery female voice.

"It's me. Who's this?"

"This is Mitzi."

"Mitzi!" I changed my tone at once. "Hi, Mitzi. How are things in alligator land?"

"Just fine. The sun is shining brightly. There isn't a cloud in the sky. It's a little muggy, that's all."

"Ugh!"

"What?"

"Oh, I just stepped on a roach."

"Well, that's New York for you. We don't have roaches here."

She means she doesn't call them that. I've seen those Florida bugs that zoom around the room like dive bombers, then scoot across the floor like black stretch limos with wings.

"Well, the weather's a little better here today, Mitzi, not like that blazing heat you're having. I guess you have to stay indoors in such weather."

"Oh, no. Chuck and I played tennis this morning and a round of golf this afternoon."

"My God, you must be burned to a crisp."

"No way," she laughed. "We love the sun. We get a real nice skin tan, sir."

Skin cancer? No, I must have heard her wrong.

"We love to be outdoors," she went on. "What do you and Lily do for exercise?"

"She jogs up and down Queens Boulevard and I go to the store."

Long pause. Then she said, "It's been nice talking to you, Joel. Could you put Lily on?"

"She isn't here. She's out helping my mother and hers shop for the wedding. Then she's bringing them back here for dinner. I'll tell her to call you."

"Don't bother. I'll call back. I have a WATTS line. Give my regards to the mothers. I'm looking forward to meeting them."

"Wait..." I started to say when I heard the key turn in the door, but Mitzi had already hung up.

In walked the three of them. Lily was loaded down with packages and I ran over to her. "Here, let me help you."

"Go away. I got them this far. I can get them to the next room and put them down."

"I was only trying to he helpful."

"Don't butter me up, Joel, just because your analyst is away and you know you've got to get along with me."

"How could you be so nasty? Didn't you have a nice day?"

"I had a ball."

"Mitzi called. She said she'd call you back. Can you imagine, she and Chuck played golf and tennis today under that blazing Florida sun!"

"What a terrible waste of time. She could have been doing what I did."

"Well, it looks like you got everything you went for. Did my mother get the shoes she wanted?"

"Of course not. She tried on twenty pairs and couldn't find one that fit."

"So what are you going to do?"

"I'll paint her old shoes silver."

"What if it rains?"

"Then they'll turn blue again. What am I, a magician?"

Lily was not in a good mood. I turned to my mother and asked, "Did you find a nice dress, Mom?"

"It's a little long."

"You have to wear a long dress for the wedding," said Lily.

"All right. After the wedding, I'll cut it down and use it for every day. You know, I'm a good seamstress."

"I know, Mom. You've made Lily some of her best clothes."

"I could have made a dress for myself but Lily said no."

"You wouldn't have finished it until after the honeymoon," said Lily.

"So what's the rush?"

Lily's mother was busy tearing open the packages.

"Did you get a nice dress?" I asked her.

"What's the difference?"

"She got a good buy," said my mother. "It was marked down three times."

"After the wedding, I'll return it," said Lily's mother.

"You can't take it back after you wear it."

"Why not? Where else can I wear it? I didn't need it in the first place."

"Then what would you wear?"

"I found Lily's wedding dress and it fits me perfectly."

"Ma!" said Lily. "You'd look like Baby Jane."

"Oh, go on. They aren't married yet. How can they have a baby? I've had enough of this. I'm going to make some hot tea. You want to help me, Bea?"

"In a minute, Frieda," my mother said. "I have to talk to Joel first."

"Something wrong, Mom?"

"Those neighbors of mine upstairs won't let me sleep. They keep moving furniture around all night and they follow me around wherever I go."

I tried to pacify her. "Ignore them, Mom. There's nothing you can do about it."

"That's what you think."

"You're not banging on the ceiling with a broom again, are you?"

"It's the only way to straighten them out."

"That's not the way to do it. They'll make trouble for you. Maybe we should try to find you another apartment."

"Why should I move out and let them get away with it?"

"To make me happy."

"I'll be happy when I straighten them out."

"Then you don't want me to be happy. You want to make yourself happy."

"Could you be happy if I'm not happy?"

How well she knew me. I watched her walk determinedly into the kitchen calling out, "I'm coming, Frieda."

Standing beside me, Lily muttered gleefully, "I'd like to punish you and leave you alone with them. But I'll wait until we take them to the wedding, like you wanted. You're going to have a real good time, Joel, and live to regret every minute of it!"

She wasn't fair. Life isn't fair. All I wanted was for everybody to be happy. Including me.

Some people find happiness in the strangest ways, as I was constantly learning from my job at *Tomorrow*. Now I was on a field assignment, covering the annual convention of the Natural Life Force Society at the Javits Center.

The place was packed with people sitting under pyramids, nibbling on grass sandwiches and having out-of-body experiences. One enterprising couple had pasted up all my UFO columns on a board and were peddling cassette tapes they claimed were made by Qrnk. I bought one to pass along to the publisher's lawyer, making sure to keep it separate from my own tapes.

Suddenly I heard my name called out on the public address system: "Joel Flom, Joel Flom, come at once to the press office!"

Oh my God!

The hysterical voice on the p.a. kept repeating "Joel Flom, come at once, come at once!" as I raced through the crowd to the press office.

"I'm Joel Flom!" I announced breathlessly. "What is it?"

"Your wife called," said the voice. "She wants you to call her right away."

I didn't like this at all.

"Can I use your phone?"

"Are you a member of the Natural Life Force Society?"

"No!"

"I'm sorry. You'll have to use the pay phone. It's just around the corridor."

Under my breath I cursed the voice and raced around the corridor, lunging for the phone just as one of the crazies was about to grab it.

"Take it easy, man, you're on another planet."

I disregarded him and reached for a quarter. I was so nervous I had to hold one hand with the other to dial the number.

"Lily? What happened?"

"I had to call Levin to find out where to reach you, Joel. He's very nice. I don't know what you're always bitching about."

"What happened!" I screamed.

"Have you got a *Valium*?"

"There's a whole bottle of *Valium* in the medicine chest. Why are you calling me for one?"

"Not for me, for you. If you have one, take it. Now."

My blood ran cold.

"I don't need a *Valium*. Just tell me what happened."

"Your mother had to go to the hospital."

"What! Wait a minute."

I reached into my shirt pocket for a *Valium* and gulped it down.

"It's nothing to get excited about, Joel. She's all right."

"Nothing? My mother's in the hospital and to you it's nothing?"

"She called her doctor because she wasn't feeling well and he had her come in for a check-up. When he examined her, he said her electricity or something wasn't right."

"An electrolyte imbalance, you mean?"

"I suppose so."

"You suppose so!"

"If you don't calm down, I'm going to hang up."

"Don't hang up, Lily. Tell me what happened."

"Nothing really. The doctor called me from his office and said he wanted your mother to spend a few days in the hospital until she's normal again. So, like the good daughter-in-law that I am, I drove down, picked her up, and checked her in. She's lucky I was home."

"She's in the hospital and you call her lucky!"

"She'll be all right."

"Don't say it."

"What should I say, she won't be all right?"
"Oomp oomp oomp."
"Oh, goodbye!"

She hung up. I just stared at the telephone, mesmerized, unable to make a decision. Finally, I realized that I had to call the doctor. My doctor.

I pulled out my wallet and fished through the cards and pictures of the kids until I found my note with Dr. Abel's number at Martha's Vineyard. Hopefully, he'd still be home and not swimming at shrink beach. I dialed the operator, telling her to charge the call to my home number.

It rang three times before somebody answered. Luck was with me so far.

"Hello. Dr. Abel?"
"Yes."
"Oh, am I glad to find you in. I hate to bother you but this is a terrible emergency."
"Who is this?"
"Joel Flom."
"Ah. What's the trouble, Mr. Flom?"
"My mother just went to the hospital."
"I'm sorry to hear that. Is she critically ill?"
"No, no. At least I don't think so. She has an electrolyte imbalance."
"Well, that can be corrected easily. Her potassium level is probably low. It's very common among the elderly."

"You don't understand, doctor. This wouldn't have happened if it wasn't for me. It's my fault."

"Your fault? You feel you should have made her eat more bananas to keep up her potassium, is that it?"

"That's not what I mean."

"What do you mean?"

"Last week a cousin of mine called. He owns all the family plots in the cemetery and he asked if I wanted to buy any. Well, I bought one."

"So now you own some real estate."

"I didn't buy it for myself, don't you understand?"

"I understand you very well."

"I should never have bought that plot. He talked me into it."

"Consider it a blessing, not a curse. You're a very caring son. God won't forget."

"But the wedding date is almost here. I want my mother to be there."

"She'll be there. I promise."

"I'm so glad you said that. It means so much more coming from you than from Lily who told me there was nothing to worry about."

"She underestimates you."

"I'm sorry I had to disturb you on your vacation."

"That's all right. You've enriched my day."

I felt so relieved when I put down the phone. What a wonderful person. A real doctor. Now I could complete my assignment with some peace of mind.

I looked around. Just a few steps away was a big pyramid with a sign proclaiming. 'Pyramid Power! Five minutes under here will bring you good fortune.'

Ridiculous! Still, it couldn't hurt to give it a try. I just won't mention it to Lily, that's all.

Of course, from Lily, I never could keep a secret. Unfortunately, when I told her that I'd sat under the pyramid, I hadn't yet turned on my tape recorder to capture her comments. They weren't very flattering.

No matter. The good news is that within a few days my mother's electrolyte imbalance was corrected and she was back home again. I saw to it that she would have plenty of bananas on hand as Dr. Abel had advised.

Time seemed to fly now that the wedding day was almost upon us. Billy and Dawn had already quit their summer jobs and Dawn had flown to Florida to be with her family. David had also quit his job, earlier than expected, when he discovered that one of the waitresses was stealing his tips.

It was great to have the kids home with me. I say with me because Lily was out shopping for specials at the supermarket and for the first time in a long while I had my sons all to myself. I felt like a real father again.

David showed me some pictures he'd taken on a hike in the Catskill when he had a few hours off. How I wished I could have been along.

"Great shots," I said. "There's nothing like being on the trail."

"What trail? It's just a little hiking path behind the hotel."

"It's still the great outdoors. The wilderness. And you know how I've always loved the wilderness."

"Dad, the closest you ever got to the wilderness is Central Park."

"Maybe so. But one of these days I'm really going to hit the trail. I've dreamed about it ever since I was a little kid."

"You're a romantic," said Billy. "One mosquito and you'd head for the nearest air-conditioned motel."

"I wouldn't go to the woods in summer. That's when I'd head for a cold climate where I could get behind a dog sled and trek my way through the frozen North, the land of Shackleton and Scott."

"I think they explored the South Pole."

"It's the same snow and ice. No heat, no humidity. Just mushing along through the trackless wastes nibbling on whale blubber. Wouldn't it be great if we could all go together, just the three of us?"

"Without Mom?"

"Naturally. She's a lady."

"Dad, that's chauvinistic," said the doctor.

"Mom's a liberated woman," said the lawyer.

"You bet she is," I said, "she doesn't have to work."

"That's the opposite of liberation."

"Not to your mother. You know, she has very strong opinions. And whatever she believes is right, to her that makes it the law of the land."

The kids laughed. Then the lawyer, who should know, agreed, "Mom does have a way of expressing her ideas like they were the law of the land."

"Yeah," said David, "like her Law of Success: 'Look hard enough and you'll find he knew somebody.'"

"Right!" I agreed enthusiastically.

That got them going. I listened, fascinated, as they reeled off some of Lily's Laws...

"The Law of Consumerism: 'Never say you don't need.'"

"The Law of Losing Things: 'Don't bother looking, it'll turn up.'"

"The Law of Second Marriages: 'If you don't spend it, his second wife will.'"

"The Law of Orderliness: 'It's better to be clean than neat.'"

"The Law of Everlasting Youth: 'By the time she's forty, every woman should have a face-lift.'"

"The Law of Life and Death: 'Don't wait until you're dead to start living.'"

We were all having a good laugh together when the door opened and Lily bustled in carrying two shopping bags stuffed with groceries.

"There's never anyone on the service elevator when your hands are full!" she exclaimed.

"The Law of Apartment House Living," I volunteered.

That made the kids howl.

"What did you say, Joel?"

"Nothing."

She turned to Billy and asked, "Did you hear from your bride-to-be while I was out?"

"Yes, Mom. She said her mother was very busy finalizing plans for the wedding. I think she's having a rough time."

"When money's no object, it can't be too rough."

"The Law of the Healthy Wealthy," said David, chuckling.

"Oh, some good news, Mom," Billy broke in quickly. "We decided what music to have at the ceremony."

"A rock band, I suppose."

"No, a string quartet."

"How chic. What will they play?"

"A little Mozart, a little Brahms."

"What, no *Alley Cat?*" I asked.

"No way, Dad."

The boys went to their room while I helped Lily empty the shopping bags so that she could prepare dinner.

"I have something to tell you, Joel. Last night, I had a terrible dream."

"You had a nightmare."

"For me it was only a dream. For you it'll be a nightmare."

"What does that mean?"

"I dreamed I went to the wedding and left you home."

"Lily! How could you do that?"

"Don't get upset, Joel. It was only a dream. Did you have a good time with the boys?"

"Yes. We talked about dodging the summer heat and humidity by taking a trip to the frozen North together and living in the great outdoors."

"You did? Well, you can count me out. That's no place for a lady."

Oh, if only the kids could have heard that!

Only the fantasy of mushing through the frozen North prevented me from passing out in the sweltering subway that kept stopping in mid-tunnel the next morning. Worse yet, I was stuck standing among an ethnic mix of Indians, Arabs, and Orientals who kept up a constant babble in strange tongues that made me feel it was I who spoke a foreign language.

I was so over-wrought that I considered getting off the train and taking a taxi right back home, then having Lily call Levin to say I had heat stroke. But I couldn't... because this was a very special day, my last day at *Tomorrow*. My summer stint was over — sooner than expected, of course, because of the wedding.

At least this day was special to me, if to nobody else. It began like most other days. 'Bama had opened the window wide, killing the air-conditioning, and this time I slammed it shut without even asking Levin's permission. I was getting cocky since I wouldn't be back again.

Besides, Levin was preoccupied bawling out Hubie for being late.

"It wasn't my fault. The subway got stuck in the tunnel," whined Hubie.

"I don't want to hear any excuses," snarled Levin. "I expect you to be here on time."

"What am I supposed to do if the subway gets stuck?"

"That's your problem."

Hubie blew his cool. He slammed his fist down on his desk rattling old coffee cups and zinging the typewriter.

"Don't do that again! If you want to let off steam, go to the shit house and slam down the terlet seat."

Hubie stormed out with Levin yelling after him, "Watch out you don't slam it down on your pecker!"

Everybody howled and Levin grinned happily.

The place was jumping. Desmond was talking on two phones simultaneously. He put one down and called out, "I may have something here, Levin. There's a fruitcake on the phone who has a poodle that can add, subtract, multiply and divide."

"Sounds like a cute story, Des. Take it down and get some pictures of the dog at a blackboard or maybe working on a computer."

Nancy was doing a story about the Kennedys and showed it to Levin. After a quick look, he said, "You missed the whole point."

"What point?" she protested. "It's just a wrap-up of the tragedies that have hit the Kennedy family, how one tragedy after another has threatened to destroy them."

"That's where you made your mistake. It's not tragedy that threatens to destroy them. It's the curse of the Kennedys. That's the angle. Play up the curse. Now do it over."

Hubie had cooled down and was back at his desk like nothing had happened. He came over to me, chuckling, "Hey, Joel, I just had a stringer tell me a medical story you wouldn't believe."

"Try me."

"Well, it seems that this gal went to see a psychoanalyst and she was so boring she put him to sleep. Then, while he was sleeping, she shot herself on his couch."

"Oh my God! Why did she go to him in the first place?"

"She was suicidal," he laughed.

"Oh, it's a joke."

"No. The stringer said it's true. Wouldn't that make a good story for us?"

I didn't think so at all. It wouldn't be fair to Dr. Abel to have a story like that in the paper. Of course, I wouldn't mention that to Hubie. What I said was, "Did you tell that to Levin?"

"No, I wanted to try it out on you first."

"Well, I don't think it's right for us, Hubie. I'd kill it and forget about it."

"Do you really think so? I hate shrinks"

"I know, but a lot of people find them helpful," I said uneasily.

"If I needed help, I'd rather go to a gypsy. They're just as good and a lot cheaper."

"But we have to consider our readers. We can't print anything that would disillusion them. Besides, we'd never get a shrink to talk to us again if we printed a story like that."

"I guess you're right, Joel. I'll kill it."

Whew! I breathed a sigh of relief. The last person I wanted to antagonize was Dr. Abel.

"Flom!"

It was Levin. He had a way of creeping up on me when I least expected it.

"I want you to look over the run-sheet," he growled, handing me a list of headlines to lead off the next issue.

"Thanks, let's have a look.

THE CURSE OF THE KENNEDYS...
ENDLESS SUPPLY OF MONEY
FROM GARBAGE...
TEN WAYS TO FRESHEN UP
A STALE MARRIAGE...
TEENIE WEENIE DIET FOR HOT DOG
LOVERS...
EXCLUSIVE: SHIRLEY MACLAINE TAKES
TANGO LESSONS FROM THE GHOST OF
RUDOLPH VALENTINO.

A very exciting lineup, Levin."

"Just be sure I get all those advance UFO columns before you leave today, Flom."

"You can have them now if you like."

"Okay. I hope you learned something about the newspaper business while you were here."

Those were his parting words. When he walked away, I dialed my friend the publisher's private phone number.

"Harold? This is Joel," I said warmly to my old college chum. "You know, this is my last day at *Tomorrow*."

"I know that, Joel. I was going to call you. You've been a great help to the paper and I hope you'll join us again whenever you feel like it. Will you? Will you think about it? Did you enjoy your work?"

"I'll never forget the experience, Harold. I'm glad you gave me this opportunity."

"You've done a great job. Have you arranged for someone else to take over the UFO column? Did you give him some ideas? Does he know where to reach that outer-space person?"

"Everything's been taken care of. I've written four advance columns just to be on the safe side and gave them to Levin."

He was very pleased and urged me again to return if I ever needed work. God forbid!

At the end of the day, everybody came over to shake my hand except Levin. He could barely conceal his pleasure at my leaving.

"I'll miss you, Joel," said Desmond. "It's been jolly good fun having you around. You really have a knack for handling fruitcakes."

Those were the last words I recorded there on tape. I felt both happy and sad as I turned off the recorder and sneaked it into my attache case. And when I closed the door behind me for the last time, I found myself thinking, "From now on, *Tomorrow* will be just another day."

For a tiny moment I had forgotten the wedding, Lily, my mother, my mother-in-law, dire eventualities too terrible to contemplate, and no Dr. Abel to smooth the way. No, in the real world, none of my tomorrows could be just another day.

I knew it. The panic was on. The days had flown by in dizzying crises as preparations for the wedding became more and more frantic. The nervousness was contagious and took its toll on everyone's digestive system. My mother was constipated, Lily's mother had diarrhea, and Lily peed so much I thought she would become dehydrated. Only the boys and I were spared. I kept my sanity by noshing on *Valium.*

At last the big moment arrived. I double-checked my supply of cassettes for the tape recorder and my tubes of sun-screen ointment. We were all of us going to take the noon flight to Florida. The boys had gone to pick up their grandmothers. Uncle Louie and Aunt Bella were coming by airport limo. Billy's two best friends who were going to be ushers would meet us at the Burmans. Dawn's maid-of-honor and her bridesmaids had already flown down.

I had reserved rooms for two nights for our side of the wedding party at an economy motel, but I had second thoughts about it.

"We should have reserved the bridal suite for ourselves," I suggested to Lily. "It would be like a second honeymoon."

"We never had a first one. Save your money, Joel. You may never work again."

"Stop that! I'm edgy enough. This is no time to upset me any further."

"Don't be upset. You're not getting married. Your son is."

"Yes, and I want him to be proud of me."

"When he sees you in a tux, he'll be proud of you."

She looked me up and down as though she'd never seen me before and said, "I must admit, you look pretty snazzy in that new suit I bought you. If I didn't know you, I might go for you."

I beamed with joy. That was the Lily I knew and loved.

"You look pretty terrific yourself in that outfit," I said. "Is that what you're going to wear on the plane?"

"No! This is what I'm going to wear at the wedding. I just wanted to try it on for you."

"You look like a million bucks, as the saying goes."

"Skip the saying. I got this for four dollars in a thrift shop."

"What! You mean it was used?"

"Probably by some fancy madam who never had it on."

"You can't wear someone else's gown to your son's wedding!"

"See how nice it looks with this shawl."

"That's second-hand too?"

"No, it used to be on Ma's piano at home. My father won it in a crap game."

"It's a *shmotta*!"

"It is not a *shmotta*. It happens to be real silk."

"But it comes from a piano."

"Where does it say that? Does it have a label that says Steinway?"

"Lily, this is our son's wedding. I don't want to be humiliated."

"You don't know what's smart."

"Mitzi's gown costs over a thousand dollars and you're going to wear a piano shawl and something that cost four bucks. There'll be very important people there."

"You don't think I'll look as good as them?"

"Better, better, believe me."

"Then stop arguing. I'm saving you money."

"All right, wear it. We'll be able to afford a better wedding present."

"You want to give them a present off my back? Oh, that's so typical of you, Joel. What you lack as a husband you want to make up for as a father."

Lily & Joel

Before I could answer, the doorbell rang and I went to open the door. Our mothers had arrived.

"I'd like a nice cup of hot tea," Lily's mother announced.

"You don't need it now," said Lily. "We'll get lunch on the plane."

"What can I eat? My teeth are killing me."

"I told you to see a gum man," my mother reminded her. "I'm going to get a little *Maalox* for myself."

"What's the matter, Mom? Don't you feel good?" I said, alarmed.

"Why shouldn't I feel good? My cholesterol's a little high, that's all."

"*Maalox* won't knock down your cholesterol."

"You've got teeth, Bea," said Lily's mother. "Eat more red meat and you'll have the strength to fight it."

They just went on and on like that. If the boys hadn't come to the rescue, I don't think we'd have gotten them out of the apartment in time to catch the plane. The boys took their grandmothers in one cab, and Lily and I took another by ourselves. This bothered me.

"I'm not sure it's fair to make the kids responsible for their grandmas," I said to Lily. "After all, they were our mothers before they became grandmothers. We mustn't forget that first and foremost they're our mothers."

"Take it from me, Joel, they'll never let us forget it. And I'll never let you forget that it was you who wanted them to come to the wedding."

Life, Love and AudioTapes

"Oomp oomp oomp."

"Oh, stop it!"

We arrived at the airport barely in time to check our bags and make the plane. Uncle Louie and Aunt Bella were already on board.

"Look at them," said Lily enviously. "No responsibilities. No mothers, no kids, no nothing."

"And nobody to love them."

"You're really sick."

When Lily's mother spotted them, she said, "You're coming too?"

"Ssshhh!" said Lily. "Sit down, Ma."

"I want to find a good seat."

"This is your seat. Sit here."

"I want to walk around a little bit."

"You can't walk around. We're going to take off."

"Strap her in, strap her in!" I growled.

"Where should I sit?" my mother asked.

"Here, here, next to Frieda."

"It's cold in here. I should have brought my sweater."

"Here, take my jacket, Mom. Don't worry."

"I'm not worried. I'm cold."

"It's 88 degrees outside."

"We're inside, not outside."

"What can I do?"

"I'm not asking you to do anything."

"Now don't get nervous when we take off, Mom."

"Why should I get nervous? You worry too much, Joel."

I checked to see that her seat belt was fastened and went over to sit beside Lily. The plane began to taxi for take-off when suddenly I remembered, "Oh my God, I never asked if they had oxygen on this flight!"

"All planes have oxygen."

"I mean extra tanks for people with heart conditions."

"Your mother will be all right."

"Oomp oomp oomp."

"I told you to stop that!"

The flight was smooth, thank God. I was worried because the weather had been bad over Florida all week, and I couldn't be sure if the pilot was paying attention to his job or screwing a stewardess in the cockpit. Fortunately, a couple of martinis helped.

Uncle Louie and Aunt Bella, gourmets to the end, had disdained the airline lunch in favor of their own brown-bagged delicacies of sturgeon on French bread and watercress with French olive oil and Balsamic vinegar. He surprised all of us by pulling a bottle of Pouilly Fuisse from a freezer bag and pouring some into our little plastic cups.

"It will help wash down that slop you're eating," he chuckled.

When the plane landed in mid-afternoon and I got off, I thought I was in hell. The heat and the humidity were overpowering. I immediately took a tube of sunscreen ointment from my pocket and rubbed it all over my face and hands.

Dawn was at the baggage whirligig to greet us. She took one look at me and laughed. "My father's waiting outside to drive you to the house and the car's air-conditioned," she said reassuringly.

I smiled gratefully.

She gave everyone a big kiss. Lily's mother looked at her, shocked. "Who are you?"

"I'm the bride."

Oh my God!

"Did you have a lot of rain here, Dawn?" Lily asked, just to distract her, I'm sure.

"Oh, it was awful. It rained all week. The ground was so wet that we had to put down a wooden floor and cover it with turf to make it look like real grass. Then we discovered that the tent was too big for the garden, so we had to cut down a whole bunch of trees to make room for it."

Lily looked at me, probably thinking of the window boxes outside our kitchen where she raised begonias. I ignored her.

Billy, David, Uncle Louie and Aunt Bella went with Dawn in her BMW. The rest of us with mothers and luggage piled into Chuck Burman's Mercedes.

He gave us a big hello and said, "It's just a short ride to the house."

"This is a very nice car," said Lily's mother, settling down into the back seat. "You're very young to have a car like this. Why don't you get one like it, Joel?"

I thought Lily would die on the spot. I thought I would die right beside her. We were both lucky. Her mother immediately conked out and took a snooze. Mine kept a quiet vigil at the window to make sure we didn't have an accident. I made foolish conversation with Chuck, hoping that the martinis would never wear off. They were the only thing that kept me sober enough to keep up a conversation and survive the drive.

The Burmans had arranged several pre-nuptial family get-togethers to introduce us to their relatives before the main event. I didn't dare venture out of our air-conditioned motel room without smearing myself with sunscreen even if it only meant racing from the lobby to an air-conditioned car. But even worse, all the parties were held outdoors in gardens or patios under what seemed to me to be a blazing sun — even though Lily kept telling me it was late, late afternoon. I had so much sunscreen on my face that everyone thought I was suffering from an advanced case of psoriasis.

By the time night came on and things cooled off a bit, we had to take our mothers back to the motel because they were becoming crazed from all the partying. So we had to forego the night-time festivities. Naturally, this made Lily furious.

The next day, the wedding day, she became positively enraged because we had to stay at the motel to look after our mothers and miss attending the rehearsal for the ceremony. I can still hear her anguished cry, "It's all your fault, Joel!" ringing in my head.

And now, with the wedding only hours away, my mother had decided that her dress was too long and she was in her room shortening the hem. Lily's mother had wandered off somewhere and Lily was frantically searching through the halls and grounds to find her.

I knew that if I didn't pull myself together somehow I'd never make it to the wedding. I needed help but there was nobody I could turn to. Everyone except us was at the rehearsal having a good time. Oh, how I needed Dr. Abel!

Suddenly, I had a brainstorm. I would make believe that Dr. Abel was here in my motel room. That's it!

I locked the door and turned down the lights. Then I rearranged two chairs in the same position as in Dr. Abel's office. On his chair I placed a pillow to represent him. I took the other chair, leaned back as I always do in his office and stared at the pillow in the dimly lit room until it took the shape of Dr. Abel. I switched on the tape recorder to make it authentic and now, as both doctor and patient, I could continue the treatment.

"I have never been so anxious in all my life," I began.

"Tell me something new."

"Lily is very angry with me."

"That's new?"

"This time it's different, doctor. She won't forgive me for insisting we bring our mothers along because they've made it impossible for us to attend the rehearsal."

"The real thing will be more exciting. They'll be there."

"That's some joke."

"It wasn't meant to be a joke, Mr. Flom. I just want to reassure you that the wedding will make up in excitement for what your wife missed by having to skip the rehearsal."

"I also want to make sure that my mother will be well and have a good, safe time at the wedding."

"You'll make sure. I guarantee it."

"You never know what will happen. Right now Lily's mother is missing and nobody knows where she is."

"Mazeltov."

"You're making me laugh, doctor."

"Laugh. You'll be happy for a change."

"This is no time to be tempting Fate."

"Why would you be tempting Fate?"

"I've never mentioned this, but years ago I made up a little jingle that I've never been able to get out of my head. Never be happy or else you'll be sad, never say anything's good or it'll be bad."

"Who said so?"

"I said so."

"You should leave those decisions to God."

"God? You believe in God?"

"What I believe doesn't matter. It's what you believe that matters."

"I believe it's dangerous to change the status quo."

"So you prefer to be miserable all the time."

"No! I want to be happy. Oomp oomp oomp."

"See how frightened you are of happiness. Your son is marrying a fine girl. Enjoy the moment. It's going to be a wedding you'll never forget."

"Never. You should see the layout Dawn's parents have on their lakefront property. They even cut down trees to make room for the tent. And because the ground was wet they put down a wooden floor and covered it with artificial turf. And they hired a chamber orchestra to provide the music, and they have three rabbis to conduct the ceremony. It's going to be like an epic, a one-shot mini-series."

"Maybe they'll televise it on PBS."

"Who knows? I'm trying to get *The New York Times* society editor to cover it."

"Good. the Burmans would be impressed."

"True, true. But... somebody's knocking at your door, doctor."

"Joel, who are you talking to in there?" yelled Lily. "Open the door!"

Startled, I remembered where I was. Dr. Abel was gone.

"Just a minute, Lily," I called back, as I rushed to turn up the lights, throw the pillow back on the bed, and return the chairs to their usual places.

When I opened the door, Lily looked at me strangely and said, "There's nobody here. Why were you talking to yourself?"

I just shrugged.

"You've been sneaking drinks," she snapped. "You can't fool me."

Ha!

For a little while I felt elated at having fooled Lily, and my spirits were buoyed up even further by my imaginary therapy session with Dr. Abel. But my good feelings didn't last. They never do. That's the story of my life. When everything seems to be going right, something always goes wrong. Lily can deny it from now until Doomsday but I know better. We'd missed attending the rehearsal and now were in danger of missing the wedding.

"Wake your mother up," I begged Lily. "Since you found her wandering around the swimming pool, she's done nothing but sleep!"

"She's up, she's up. Worry about your mother. She's in worse shape."

"Oh my God, what's the matter with her?"

"Nothing. She's just taking a bath."

"Now? We'll miss the wedding!"

"Tell her that, Joel."

I ran to my mother's room. She was out of the tub and drying her hair in a towel. I pleaded with her, "Please, Mom, get ready already, or we'll be late for the wedding."

"I can't rush, Joel. I'm not as young as you. I have to dry my hair."

"How could you get your hair wet in the bathtub?"

"I turned on the shower by mistake. All I wanted was to take a bath."

"Why did you have to bathe now?"

"When should I bathe? After the wedding?" She had a way of making the ridiculous sound reasonable. All I could do was to yell, "Lily! Come and help my mother. Her hair is wet."

We finally managed to get her presentably dressed, and both of them out of the motel, and into the limo waiting to take us to the Burmans' home.

"This is only the beginning," Lily said. "Keep your fingers crossed, Joel, and maybe we'll manage to get through the ceremony. Then maybe we'll manage to get through the reception."

"Don't talk that way, Lily. You make me nervous."

"I'm warning you, you'd better keep an eye on my mother!"

"Your mother? What about mine?"

"You're man enough to look after both of them."

"But I have to watch what my mother eats."

"Let me watch her. You watch mine. If you don't, she's sure to do something to embarrass us in front of all those fancy guests."

"They'll understand."

"They will? When she stuffs the silver in her handbag to take home as souvenirs?"

"Oh, no!"

"Oh, yes. Napkins, ashtrays, leftovers, no telling what. You know her."

"All right, I'll watch her."

We were the last to arrive. All the guests were already seated inside the tent, waiting for the ceremony to commence. Mitzi and Chuck greeted us warmly, and everybody kissed everybody else like they do in the Academy Awards TV specials.

"Glad you could make it," said Mitzi, laughing.

I grinned, to be sociable, all the while keeping an eye on my mother who was looking around at the big house, the lake, the string orchestra in the enormous tent that was decorated from top to bottom with flowers of every description.

"So this is Hollywood," she said. "I always told you, Joel, that you should go to Hollywood. I'm glad you took my advice."

I just scrunched up, nodding my head idiotically. I kept a weather eye on Lily's mother who was telling Dawn's father, "You look very nice, and you're marrying a very nice girl."

"Thank you," he said, "but I'm not the groom. Your grandson, Billy, is the groom."

"Oh? Well, you'll find somebody. You look very nice."

"You look very nice too."

"I'm shot."

My brain cells were raging from the mothers and the unbelievable heat and humidity. But under the tent, thank God, the fans were blowing as Dawn had promised, and it was a blessed relief. The ushers, Billy's friends from college, led us to our seats.

"They look like *goyim*," said Lily's mother.

"Sssshhhh!" said Lily. "They are *goyim*, nice Gentile boys from their law school."

"Where's the draft coming from?" my mother asked.

"Probably from the fans, Mom. Here, let me sit on this side of you. I'll shield you."

"What a son," said Lily. "I hope I have it as good from my sons."

"Not now, Lily, please!"

The three rabbis took their places. The more than 150 guests stopped coughing and talking. The string orchestra began to play Pachelbel's *Canon*.

"That's opera music," my mother said.

"It's the wedding march," said Lily's mother.

I wished I had a drink.

Everybody's eyes turned when Billy came walking down the aisle with David, his best man.

"My little boys," said Lily. "Look at them in their tuxes. Only yesterday they were playing basketball in the playground."

Then came the bridesmaids with the maid of honor, and Dawn, the radiant bride, on the arm of her father.

"That's a hand-made gown she's wearing," said my mother. "I have material just like it at home that she could have had."

"Who is that man?" asked Lily's mother.

"That's her father. You were just talking to him." I whispered.

"Why aren't you up there?"

"Sssshhh!"

The ceremony was short, thank God, with each of the three rabbis saying a few words. When Billy crushed the glass with his heel, Lily muttered, "I'll bet that was Waterford crystal."

After the ceremony, a dozen waiters came out of nowhere pouring champagne. I took my first glass in a gulp like an *Alka-Seltzer*.

"Take a look at Uncle Louie," said Lily. "He's checking the bottle to see if it's good stuff."

"Take my word for it, Lily, it's good stuff."

"What do you care as long as it's got alcohol in it! Behave yourself, Joel."

I wasn't listening. I was watching my mother. She was about to drink a whole glass of champagne.

"No, no, Mom," I said, drinking half of it myself. "Don't drink this, you'll get sick."

By the time I turned around to check up on Lily's mother, she had downed a full glass.

"Lily!"

"I know, I know. I warned you, Joel!"

She took the glass away from her mother and said, "That's enough, Ma."

"I'm having a good time. Leave me alone."

"You're getting drunk."

"Oh, go on!"

I needed help. I spotted David with a can of beer in his hand and went over to him. "Do me a favor, please, David. Keep an eye on your grandmothers so your mother and I can circulate around, okay?"

"Sure, Dad. Don't worry about a thing. Have a good time."

No wonder he's an honor student.

Minutes later, everything was set up under the tent for the dinner. And what a dinner! Fresh paté flown in from Paris, hearts of palm, filet mignon — and for my mother who had trouble swallowing, there was sole amandine. Later came a pastry table that seemed as long as a football field.

The highest praise for the meal came from Uncle Louie who proclaimed afterwards, "Tonight we dined."

Between the champagne and the wine served with the dinner I was, as the *goyim* say, feeling no pain. And to make sure I stayed that way, I had a few brandies afterward.

"Where's your mother?" Lily asked me.

"David's looking after her. Where's your mother?"

"Over there, sleeping in her chair."

"Good."

And it all seemed too, too good to be true, and I was definitely feeling too good to question anything. Lily and I went over to Billy and Dawn to kiss them and wish them good luck. Lily said wistfully, "It was such a beautiful wedding. I just wish we could do it all over again."

Dawn had an answer. "If you have a VCR, you can play it back on your TV set. It's all on videotape. Didn't you notice the camera following you around?"

"No."

Oh, my God, I thought, now the whole Burman clan would be able to spot Lily's mother swiping the silverware!

"Hey, look at Grandma," said Billy. "She's drinking from a bottle!"

I turned to look at my mother. She was sipping *Maalox*. Frantic, I ran to her and almost screamed, "Mom, are you all right?"

"Don't get so excited, Joel," she said. "I'm just a little bloated, that's all. You worry too much."

I took another long sip of brandy.

"Joel, who's that man Chuck Burman's talking to?" Lily asked me. "He looks very familiar."

"That's Don Shula, the Miami Dolphins' coach! How about that, Lily, he's a friend of Chuck's. Wowie!"

"He probably gives him free parking space in one of his parking lots."

"I don't care. Just seeing him here makes me feel... somehow diminished."

"You are diminished."

"So what should I say if anyone asks me what I do for a living?"

"Tell them you're retired."

"I'm too young to retire."

"No one will ever know."

"I'll tell them I work at *Tomorrow*."

"You do that and I'll deny I'm married to you."

"So you're ashamed of my having worked there, right?"

"No, I'm not ashamed. But Dawn's family might be."

"That's too fucking bad!"

"Calm down, Joel. That's the way life is and you have to accept it. Also you're drunk."

"Dr. Abel wouldn't like your attitude."

"Well, he isn't here. It's just you and me and Dawn's rich relatives. Accept things as they are, Joel, and stop fighting Fate."

She was right. So I joined her in being pleasant, shaking strange hands, and kissing cheeks of nameless people, knowing all the while that they were richer than we were or ever would be.

"These guys aren't wearing rented tuxedos like me," I said to Lily.

"So what? If you didn't have a credit card, you'd be in a plain blue suit. Look at it that way. And just remember one thing, which is more important than anything else."

"What?"

"Mitzi served bread at the dinner. I was right all along, wasn't I?"

"You sure were."

Of course. She's always right. Still, I was delighted to see a big smile on her face. I mean, it takes so little to make Lily happy. And when she's happy, I'm happy. Maybe that's why our marriage has endured all these years.

I made a mental note to take it up with Dr. Abel when he returned after Labor Day, which was practically here. I could hardly wait. And this time I might play some of the tapes for him so that he could hear for himself how I coped with all the crises I had to endure. He might love to hear the imaginary session I had with him in the motel. He could correct what I did wrong, just as he would a test paper. He might even grade it.

Wouldn't it be nice to get an "A" from Dr. Abel? Oh, wow!

*U*ntil Labor Day arrived I was in a near state of collapse. A month of crisis after crisis without Dr. Abel had taken its toll. The summer was ending as it had begun with another record-breaking rise in the THI. Even the air-conditioner was sweating under the strain of keeping the apartment cool and dry.

I was walking around in my shorts and Lily was standing by the window wearing only a thin housecoat. I got all charged up looking at her figure silhouetted against the sunlight shining through the flimsy cotton. But as soon as she caught me ogling her, she moved away and snapped, "For shame, you dirty old man!"

I didn't answer or try anything because I could see she wasn't in the mood for a sexual encounter. I had to be careful because all we had now were each other. David had gone back to his prestigious medical school. Billy and Dawn would soon return to their prestigious law school after their honeymoon. My mother was back in her apartment, remodeling her wedding dress so she could wear it to the supermarket and her doctor's office. Lily's mother had successfully returned her wedding dress and was back home sipping hot tea and massaging her gums with the tea bag.

I had no job and no writing assignments. I must have looked depressed because Lily came over to me and said, "Stop feeling sorry for yourself, Joel."

"You're right."

"There'll be plenty of time for that when your brain corrodes from drinking and you can't write any more."

"That's mean!"

"I'm a realist. I'm used to having things go wrong in my life, so if they get worse it's no big deal. But you have to have everything going your way, so you drink when it doesn't."

"I take a little nip once in a while, that's all, and you know it."

"Listen, Joel, you've got plenty to be thankful for. We managed to get through the wedding. Our mothers are back home safe and sound, at least as sound as they'll ever be. And the kids are healthy and happy."

I rapped the table hard with my knuckles.

"Don't knock wood!"

"If I want to knock wood, I will. If it bothers you, that's your problem."

"I can't stand it when you do that. I feel like I've said something evil."

"Well, that's one way of looking at it."

"All I said were good things."

"That's another way of looking at it."

"Oh, I can't wait for you to see your analyst."

"Neither can I. Just one more day and he'll be back in his office for my appointment."

The telephone started ringing. It caught me by surprise and I began rapping the table again.

"Don't do that!" said Lily. "It's only the phone."

She picked it up, then held it out to me. "It's him, your guru."

Dr. Abel?

My hands shook as I took the phone and I couldn't stop my voice from quivering as I asked anxiously, "Dr. Abel? Are you all right?"

"I'm fine, thank you, Mr. Flom. But, unfortunately, I'm going to be delayed getting back to my office so I have to put off our appointment for a week. Is that all right with you?"

"Oh, absolutely. Definitely. But there's something I must tell you now."

I waved to Lily to go into another room, then whispered into the phone, "Listen, Dr. Abel, I had a very disturbing dream last night."

"About the wedding?"

"No, the wedding went fine actually, just as you said it would. I dreamt I was in a movie theatre and everyone around me, wherever I looked, was smiling. Then suddenly it struck me that all of them, every one of them, were wearing masks!"

He began to laugh.

"They weren't wearing masks, Mr. Flom. You were. Your whole life is theatre and the legendary masks of comedy and tragedy are indistinguishable to you. That's why you find every smile suspect, as you did in your dream. We'll go over it again when I see you next week."

I put down the phone in a daze.

"You don't look very happy," said Lily, coming back into the room when she heard me hang up. "Did your analyst quit you?"

"He can't see me until next week. He's extending his vacation for another week."

"Sure, he probably found a girlfriend half his age and wants to make the most of it."

"Lily! I feel bad enough. Don't make me feel worse."

"What's such a big deal, waiting another week? That's a catastrophe?"

I nodded despondently.

"Don't feel sad," she said. "You've still got me."

A perfect ending.

*N*ot so fast, Joel! This is your Lily talking now, into your trusty tape recorder. After you hauled me into bed and I discovered that you'd been taping our very private life, I was terribly shocked, as you know. But I let you talk me into exposing our private life as a public service.

Well, after Labor Day when your guru returned and things got back to normal, I read every word of your transcribed tapes and your running commentary.

It was hard for me to believe that this is how you view our relationship. But like I said earlier, since it's smart these days to let it all hang out, I decided not to let it bother me. You can offer it for publication. What I never suspected was that you would dare offer first publication rights to your old college chum, the publisher of *Tomorrow!*

When you told me... ecstatically, yet... that he was eager to feature it, I couldn't believe it. A book is one thing, but splashing our love life across the front page of *Tomorrow* in lurid headlines is something else.

You expect too much of me, Joel. I was so worked up about this shocking development that I had a tremendous need to talk to someone about my feelings. But to who? Or to whom, as William Safire would say?

It was no use talking to you. Your mind was made up. For the first time in my married life I wasn't sure how to handle my feelings. There was only one person to talk to, the one who was responsible for all this. I had to swallow my pride and talk to Dr. Abel myself!

Well, I don't know how you find it so easy to talk to that man. I was a bundle of nerves just contemplating talking to him, yet I had to talk to him because I *was* a bundle of nerves.

When I phoned him and said I was Lily Flom, he made a strange sound, like he was choking on something, and I told him at once I would pay him for his time on the telephone.

"No, no, Mrs. Flom, that won't be necessary," he said. "But why are you calling me? Is your husband ill?"

"He's fine, Dr. Abel. It's me who's sick."

"You?"

He spoke in that soft psychiatric voice those people have but I didn't understand why he seemed so surprised that it was I who could be sick.

"I want you to know right away, Dr. Abel, that I'm taping this conversation."

"Good. Perhaps you'll have another chapter for your book."

"Ah, so you admit that you put Joel up to this business of taping our private lives and publishing it as a book!"

"I understand, Mrs. Flom, that he has also taped other people as well, various relatives, his co-workers, even his sessions with me, because all such conversations help give him insight into the way he thinks and conducts his life."

"That's all very nice, for him. But what about me?"

"This book will benefit you as much as it will him, I promise you."

"But what you don't know, Dr. Abel, is that Joel has offered the book to the tabloid, *Tomorrow*, and they're going to condense it and feature it on the front page!"

"*Mazeltov.*"

"What? You don't find that objectionable? An insult?"

"Not if they pay well for that insult, and I have a hunch that they will."

"But these tapes reveal some of the most intimate details of our life together. It could be very embarrassing to be on the front page of a sensational newspaper."

"You'll be in good company, Mrs. Flom. You'll share headlines with famous celebrities. You and Joel will become famous by the mere process of association and will sell thousands of books as a result of the publicity."

He made it all seem so rational that I began to understand why Joel never questioned his advice. Still, I wasn't convinced.

"I understand what you're saying, Dr. Abel, but I can't help feeling ashamed, that's why I've called you."

"Be proud, not ashamed. Remember, Mrs. Flom, those tapes reveal your husband's passionate love for you."

"Even in the pages of *Tomorrow?*"

"Yes."

"You really feel it's right for Joel to publish such personal matters over his name?"

"Oh, no, that would be wrong."

"Ah, so you agree with me."

"It should be published over both your names."

"Both our names? You mean I should be a co-author?"

"Absolutely. It's your story as well as his. And together you will proclaim your love to all the world."

"Maybe we should sign a collaboration agreement!" I couldn't help saying sarcastically.

"You already have. It's called a marriage license... Mrs. Flom, are you still there?"

"Yes, Dr. Abel. I'm just a little flabbergasted. I mean, maybe you're right, we should collaborate. But if we do, shouldn't my name come first?"

Life, Love and AudioTapes

"Why not?" he said with one of those chuckles Joel used to tell me about. "I'm sure your husband would want it that way."

Of course he would. That's my Joel, and Dr. Abel knew it. It made me feel better. It's like I said when I first learned about the tapes, "After twenty-five years of marriage, are there really any secrets left?"

Poor dear Joel, whom I love and abhor. You are foolish, sentimental and depraved. But how comforting it is to sleep each night beside a man of unpredictable passions.

So the hell with the tapes. Play them anywhere, any time. And the hell with *Tomorrow*. Publish them there or anywhere. For we do have a love story worth telling, don't we?

A perfect ending, like you said.